Dream Team

hotshots

TERENCE BLACKER

MACMILLAN CHILDREN'S BOOKS

First published 1997 by Pan Macmillan Children's Books
a division of Macmillan Publishers Limited
25 Eccleston Place, London SW1W 9NF
and Basingstoke

Associated companies throughout the world

ISBN 0 330 32915 4

1 3 5 7 9 8 6 4 2

A CIP catalogue record for this book is available from
the British Library.

Phototypeset by Intype London Ltd
Printed by Mackays of Chatham plc, Kent

For Stephanie Blacker

Acknowledgement

I would like to thank Michelle Dunk of Tonbridge, Kent, for The Pilchard.

Dear Stevie

It was delightful to hear from you after all this time. Your letter took me back to those strange summer days in Oakmere which changed so many lives.

I would, of course, be delighted to say "a few words" to introduce you and the Hotshots. For the reasons you know about (!!!), my memories of the Oakmere Tournament are a bit hazy but I'm sure your version of Broadhurst Comprehensive's most successful football team's visit to the countryside will be tremendously interesting and valid.

What would you like me to say in my introduction?

Yours affectionately

D. (Mrs!)

PS I wouldn't include any of the "problems" with the police.
PPS Or that horrid Bigstuff and his biking thugs.
PPPS Not to mention the "love element"!
PPPPS And I'd gloss over the unpleasantness at the manor. Least said, soonest mended!
PPPPPS Football, summer, fun – keep it positive, eh Stevie?
PPPPPPS Or maybe you should just tell the story in your own way . . .

CHAPTER ONE

Call me Miss Responsible

Here's where it all began.

I was way late with some homework. I had just gagged down a truly barfworthy school dinner and was on my way back to the classroom when Miss Baker, the head teacher's secretary, loomed up out of the dweebs and losers who were hanging out in the corridor and told me that Mr Morley wanted to see me.

"Could I call in after class, Miss Baker?" I asked politely. "I've got to finish this super-urgent—"

"Now."

Yeah. Right. Thanks for being so understanding.

So there I was, moments later, being led into the holy of holies, Mr Morley's study.

"Stevie Rostand for you, Mr Morley," Miss Baker intoned before fading away like some grey ghost so thin that she can appear and disappear through the crack in the door.

"Ah, Stevie. Take a pew, will you?"

"Hullo, Mr Morley." I walked to the guest chair and sat down with the old ring-of-confidence smile you see in the toothpaste ads. Fact is, apart from being late with homework (and getting later by the second, thank you very much, Mr Morley), I hadn't actually done anything wrong.

Or had I?

Moonie Morley (so called because the top of his head is like a big pale moon) looked up and took off his specs with a dramatic twitch of the head. He leant back in his chair, and crossed his legs and his arms at the same time. Body-language-wise, it was not a promising start.

"So. Stevie Rostand." The head teacher broke the silence eventually.

"Yup. That's me." I was not going to let Moonie break me down with the old long silence routine.

"How are the Hotshots?"

"Cool." I shrugged. "Well, they're kind of ex-Hotshots right now, I guess. Our manager's got a job. We haven't played together for six months. I guess we've all developed different interests from football."

"Interests? What sort of interests?"

I thought of our ex-team. Lisa was into acting, Ellie was into the environment, Eve was into music, Roberta and Charlie were into boy-craziness and Tara – I didn't even want to think about what Tara was getting into.

"Like work, living, growing up?" I said carefully. "The usual stuff, you know?"

"Shame about that." The head teacher sat forward and, just as I was thinking, *Yeah, like you've always been a really big supporter of the Hotshots*, he picked up a letter from his desk. "You've been invited to take part in a tournament in East Anglia. I thought it would be rather fun."

"How? Why? Who? I mean – tournament?"

"Mrs Fairbrother put forward the Hotshots' name for something called the Oakmere Tournament."

I was getting confused. "Who's Mrs Fairbrother?" I asked.

Moonie gave a weary, trials-of-a-head-teacher smile. "She's a very kind woman who happens to be a governor of Broadhurst Comprehensive. Ever since the Hotshots did so well in the Metropolitan Cup, she's taken a great interest in your progress."

It was my turn to smile. I hadn't been part of the team when it was first set up but, so far as I could gather, no one at Broadhurst – not Moonie, not the teachers, and certainly not the school governors – had been exactly bowled over by the idea of a girls' football team. But then I guess success can change people's minds.

"Her family come from that part of the world," Moonie continued. "In fact, she has very kindly suggested you might like to stay with her mother for three days before the tournament – make it a little holiday in the country for all of you."

"All seven of us? Where does she live – like a hotel?"

"It's a manor." Morley spoke as if it was obvious that Mrs Fairbrother's mum couldn't live in anything but a manor.

"It sounds great but . . . where's the catch?"

"So young and yet so cynical." Morley smiled. "It's just a way of thanking you girls for all the good publicity the Hotshots have brought to Broadhurst. Not every act of generosity has to have a catch."

"I guess not," I said, not entirely convinced. "Can I check it out with the others?"

"Of course." Morley put on his spectacles. "Let me know by tomorrow," he said.

"Um, Mr Morley." I stood up, but hesitated for a moment. "Why have you asked me? Lisa's the captain and Eve does all the organizing and Charlie—"

"I've been most impressed by the way you've adapted to life at Broadhurst, given your . . . background."

"Being American, you mean?"

"Partly that. Although by now I see you more as an honorary Brit."

"Gee, thanks a bunch," I murmured.

Moonie laughed. "No, it's simply because you're a responsible person." He reached for his pen and started writing, as if I were no longer in the room.

Seconds later, I was out of there. I stood in the corridor, too amazed to speak.

By chance, Lisa and Ellie were wandering down the corridor, making their way back to class.

"Hey, what happened?" Lisa looked at me as I stood there like a stunned goldfish.

"Have you had bad news?" Ellie asked.

I looked from one to the other, still kind of out of it. "Moonie just called me a responsible person."

"That's nice," said Ellie.

"Oh yeah, right. Like I'm some kind of school sad case all of a sudden. I've never been so insulted in all my life."

They both laughed and moved away.

"But hey – " I ran after them, "there was something else . . ."

*

5

Bottom line, no one was exactly drop-dead crazy about the idea of going out to the country when school broke up.

Or at least almost no one.

Somehow I managed to get the Hotshots together after school that day. While we were waiting for Tara, who was late as usual, I mentioned Moonie's idea that the Hotshots might hit the comeback trail this summer holidays.

The reaction went like this:

Lisa: I think I'm auditioning for a Christmas catalogue. (Note to the reader: This is no big deal – Lisa is always auditioning for something. In fact, life is an audition for Lisa.)

Ellie: Oh no, that's the week of the big whale rally in Trafalgar Square. (Note to the reader: Whales are not actually rallying here – their job is to be saved by Ellie.)

Roberta: I was hoping for a bit of quality time with Dom. (Note to the reader: Dom is Dumbo Dominic of Year Three. Quality time with Dominic? Puhlease!)

Eve: Actually, I was booked to go on this piano course. (Note to the reader: Eve's parents are so ambitious for her it makes your teeth ache just to see them – boy, are those guys in for a disappointment.)

Charlie: I'll be asleep for the first few days of the holidays. (Note to the reader: This is true – maybe because she's growing so fast, Charlie zonks out at every possible moment.)

So the conversation drifted off to clothes and boys and what everyone was doing that particular weekend. I managed to play the good ole Sunny Stevie act but some little voice inside me was going, hullo, whatever happened to the Hotshot team spirit? Didn't we have the rest of the summer to do all these other things? A few days in the country – a few laughs, a bit of football, maybe even some sunshine. Was that so horrendous?

"Hullo, ding-dong, anyone at home?" Lisa nudged me. "You haven't spoken for a whole minute. Are you ill?"

"No, I'm good."

There was something about my voice. They all looked at me.

"Uh-oh, she's in lurve," said Roberta.

"Get real," I snapped. "There's more to life than boys."

"You want to go, don't you?" said Roberta. "You're disappointed about this tournament thing."

"Nah." I gave a little smile. "I'm going back to the States for the summer with my parents anyway. It's no big deal. Like, Hotshots – who cares?"

There was a slightly embarrassed silence, as if we were each of us guilty of a small act of betrayal.

"We don't have a manager," muttered Charlie.

There was another silence.

"Who needs a manager?" said Lisa. "We could manage ourselves – if we were going. Which we're not."

"Maybe Dom could come with us," murmured Roberta shyly. "If Dom was there, I'd—"

It was while we were trying to explain to Roberta why taking Dom with us wasn't such a great idea and suggesting – in our own gentle, caring way – that maybe it was time she considered getting a life, when Tara appeared, complaining about getting yet another detention for talking in class. (Note to the reader: Collecting detentions is Tara's private hobby.)

We stopped talking, each of us aware that we had reached a decision without consulting Tara. She was shovelling some gross chocolate bar into her mouth when she looked at us.

"Washmatter?" she said, chewing. "Did someone die?"

The others looked at me.

"It was just . . . we were talking about this tournament in the country at the beginning of the summer holidays and how the Hotshots had been invited," I said quietly. "We'd decided that—"

"Oh yesss!" Tara punched the air with her right hand. "The Hotshots back in action. And I was just thinking what a drag summer was going to be."

It was Lisa who started, catching Charlie's eye, burying her face in her hands. Soon all of us were laughing. It was as if Tara – big, clumsy, innocent Tara – had expressed the feelings that each of us had been trying to ignore while we were acting so cool and grown-up.

I guess at that moment we all knew that we were on our way.

"What's the joke?" said Tara angrily. "What's your problem, you guys?"

Roberta shrugged. "We were thinking that maybe it wasn't such a great idea."

"What? *What*?"

I glanced at the others and smiled. "Let's just talk this one through, shall we?" I said.

So we did.

CHAPTER TWO

I Get Unglued

"Oakmere."

"Yup."

"East Anglia."

"Uh-huh."

"All the Hotshots."

"Except Jamie. He's on like some park-keeping course."

It was dinner. My parents sat at each end of the dining-room table, all dark suits and disapproval. It's kind of a tricky moment when they both get back from the office – I guess they need to tune back into being parents after a day of top-level executive ditsing about at the bank where they work – but that night I forgot and just came out with the news about the return of the Hotshots.

OK, so I goofed. What else is new?

"Stevie." My father nodded slowly, as if making some big boardroom decision. "I hate to drizzle on your parade, honey, but I just wonder whether it's entirely appropriate for you to be waltzing around East Anglia with . . . those girls."

"Hullo, I'm like thirteen years old, Daddy. It's not as if

I'm going to some rave and taking loads of drugs and running round with boys."

"That's quite enough of that, Stevie," said my mother, who thinks that saying something is almost as bad as doing it.

"You'd be surprised at some of the things which go on in the country," said my father. "It's not all cheery red-faced sons of toil bringing in the harvest, you know."

"It's a football tournament," I protested. "We're staying with the mother of a school governor. In a manor. What could go wrong?"

Juan, the guy who looks after us, came in at this point and a tense family silence descended on the room until he had left with the plates.

"I'm afraid we wouldn't be able to accompany you," said my mom.

"No?" I almost managed to sound surprised.

"The office doesn't run itself." My father dabbed at his mouth with a napkin as he repeated this favourite line of his. "In the real world, not everything stops for football."

"Tell me about it," I murmured.

"Who would be in charge of you?" asked my mother. "If you go, that is."

I winced. Gerry Phelan, the manager who took us to the final of the Met Cup, was working these days. Lisa had rung him after school and begged, pleaded, him to help us one more time, but Gerry couldn't do it. As for the Hotshots' parents or older brothers or sisters, none were likely to impress my parents with their general competence. "I haven't worked that out yet," I said.

Suddenly on each side of me, my parents were staring at me as if I had just turned into a Martian or something.

"I?" said Mom.

"I wasn't aware you were team captain," said my father.

"If you must know, Morley talked to me first because he thought I was responsible," I snapped. "I'm sorry but, for a moment, I forgot I was meant to be like Little Miss Nobody. Just for a second – for a tiny second – I had this crazy idea that the head teacher was right and I could organize something for myself. But thanks, Mom, thanks, Daddy – thanks for putting me right. I must have been crazy. I'll tell them all to forget it."

OK, I guess I kind of came unglued there – but at least I came unglued with style. As I swept out of the room, I couldn't help feeling the small sense of triumph of the worm that has turned.

I was sitting on my bed, staring out of the window, when moments later, there was a nervous knock on my door.

Mom came in, sat on the bed, put a hand on my shoulder. "We didn't mean to dent your self-esteem, honey," she said softly.

I shrugged her hand away. "What esteem? What self?" I said. "I guess I'm not big enough to have a self yet, am I? I can't even be trusted to arrange a game of football with my friends."

"Did Mr Morley really ask you to organize it?"

"Sure he did. Amazing as that might seem to you."

"All right. I guess you can go to the tournament," Mom said eventually. "So long as you have an adult along with you." The hand went back to my shoulder. "All right?"

"Sure," I muttered.

"Maybe a parent. Or a teacher."

"As if. Who's going to want to spend the first week of the summer holidays looking after the Hotshots?"

My mother smiled. "Search me, honey," she said. "You're in charge."

"Excellent. Well done, Stevie."

Moonie Morley ran a hand across his pale scalp. "For one moment, I thought I was going to have to send the boys' team."

"No, we're really up for it," I said.

"Fine. I'll tell Mrs Fairbrother. Now, because the school was involved in setting up this trip, I'll need to let the parents know that Gerry Phelan will be in charge."

"Ah." I winced. "Bit of a problem there. Gerry has to work. And none of the parents can make it. We were wondering if an adult from the school could come along."

"At the beginning of the holidays? You might have a problem there."

"I'll ask around."

"Good girl. Shut the door behind you."

We put the word around among the teachers.

The word came back.

It was "no".

Not that anyone put it quite like that. The replies were more of the "Oh dear, I really would have liked to come with you but I have to go to Scotland for a wedding/get into training for this charity run/write my novel/babysit my auntie's goldfish. What a pity. If only . . ."

Yeah yeah.

In the end, help came from the most unlikely source imaginable. The library.

It happened that Eve Simpson's idea of a good time was to sit around in the library during dinner break, doing her homework and reading books. Sometimes, just to give her brain a rest for a few seconds, she would chat to the school librarian, Miss Billingham, a quiet, pale woman whom you'd never notice unless you were really looking. They'd rap about books and poems and, er, poems and books.

The day after I had told the head teacher that the Hot-shots were up for a trip to the country, Eve mentioned our problem to Miss Billingham.

Politely, the librarian asked where the tournament was.

A place called Oakmere, Eve had said.

And suddenly, according to Eve, Miss Billingham's face had turned the deepest shade of scarlet. "Oakmere?" she asked. "Near Ipswich?"

"That's right," said Eve. "Now the book I was looking for is . . ."

Fast forward thirty minutes. Eve was sitting there, deep into chapter two. Suddenly Miss Billingham was beside her, chatting absent-mindedly about the tournament.

"I suppose you need a real football coach for your trip?" she said.

"Not really." Eve kept reading. "Just a responsible adult."

13

The librarian wandered off. Three paragraphs later, she was back.

"I know Oakmere," she said.

"Yes? What's it like?"

"Nice." Miss Billingham seemed to be blushing again. "Very nice indeed."

Slowly – and, for a bright girl, Eve can be very slow – an idea percolates through to her brain.

"I suppose you wouldn't consider helping us," she said.

"Me? Well, no, I really . . . but if you thought . . . I hadn't considered . . . Oh, all right then."

Moments later, Eve had reported the news to Lisa and me.

"Miss Billingham at a football tournament?" Lisa shook her head in disbelief. "Er, no. I don't think so."

We talked about it for a while. Miss B knew nothing about football.

But who cared?

She was extremely nervous.

So?

She hardly ever said a word to anyone.

What was this – the Oakmere Conversation Tournament?

"I think she could be all right," I said finally. "At least she won't cause us any trouble."

It's true, that's what I said. I mean, how was I to know about the Secret Life of Miss Billingham?

CHAPTER THREE

The Thing from Planet Sad

I'll spare you the grim details of what happened between the day we agreed to enter the Hotshots for the tournament at Oakmere and the end of term.

– How Lisa's mum wanted to come along with us because she once appeared in this darling film up that way and she did so want to relive the memories. (Er, no.)

– Or how Charlie's dad took her to the doctor's to check what jabs she should have before going to the country. (Would you believe, none?)

– Or how the boys tried to enter their team in the Oakmere tournament and were even sent the forms so that all they needed was a simple bit of organization. (But not simple enough for the boys.)

– Or how we tried to persuade Jamie O'Keeffe to come and told him that he was our special Hotshots mascot and that it wouldn't be the same without him but how in the end he preferred to go on a course about how to look after ponds. (Gee thanks, Jamie.)

– Or how Ellie's family all but had a group nervous breakdown when it was discovered she wouldn't be there for this big deal of a wedding anniversary her grandparents were having and that she seemed to think that football was more important than family. (Too right it is.)

– Or even how Mr Williams, Tara's dad, decided at the last minute that the school should pay for her train ticket, that he wasn't swearing well going to pay out of his own swearing pocket for a swearing school trip, that his daughter was such a brilliant daughter she should be paid for but he certainly wasn't going to swearing buy the ticket, and how the school luckily agreed to pay for Tara at the last minute. (Doesn't sound quite right, does it? In fact, it wasn't the school, it was a "mysterious secret benefactor". Thanks, Daddy.)

No, I'm certainly not going to tell you about all that.
   Let's go . . .

The first shock to await us when Ellie, Eve and I arrived at the school gates the Tuesday after the end of term was that there, standing next to Miss Billingham, was a middle-aged hippy type in old jeans, T-shirt and trainers.
   As we drew closer, we saw that this tragic, baggy sight with all its bulges in the wrong places was none other than the Moonie Man himself, Mr Morley.

16

"Hi, Hotshots," he said, doing a sort of wibble-wobble dance for a couple of seconds. "I was just out jogging and I thought I'd see you all off."

"I never knew you were a jogger," said Eve in her cutest, goodie-two-shoes voice.

Moonie rolled his shoulders in a way which set his lardy pecs flapping in the wind. "I like to keep in shape," he said.

"You wish," I murmured under my breath.

Charlie and Roberta appeared from around the corner. Two steps behind them was Lisa – new hair, new tracksuit and chatting away, all mock casual, on a mobile telephone. We hadn't left home and already the team show-off was on top form.

"Right, OK," she was going. "Don't forget to record *Neighbours*, bye." She clicked the little phone shut and tucked it into a top pocket. "Hi!" she said brightly.

"A mobile phone?" Ellie's voice was heavy with disapproval.

"Stevie had one on a school trip once," said Lisa moodily.

"That belonged to my parents," I said angrily. "It was for emergencies."

"Mine too."

"What, like recording *Neighbours*?" said Eve. "You are such a poser, Lisa."

It was then that, in a rare – no, unique – instance of good timing, Tara made her entrance, the big black van owned by Mr Williams screeching to a halt across the road from where we stood. The radio was blaring and from the back of the van came the sound of an army of children fighting. The front passenger door slid open. Tara emerged, her hair and clothes looking wilder than ever. A few words – mostly swear words – could be heard from inside the van. Then her bag was thrown out, and the van roared off.

Tara picked up the bag, as if this was the way anyone arrived, and ambled across the road to where we were standing.

"Hey, what's happening?" She stopped suddenly when she saw the head teacher in jogging gear. "Sheesh," she said. "It's the Thing from Planet Sad."

There was one of those awkward moments that tend to follow Tara and which everyone except her seems to notice.

"Yes, well." Morley was looking like a man who wished he had stayed in bed. "You girls have a train to catch." He gave a little wave, turned and jogged off down the road.

"What a mover," said Roberta.

"Get those legs," laughed Lisa.

"That sweaty T-shirt, man." Tara spoke in her loudest voice. "It goes beyond."

I glanced at Miss Billingham but she was looking in the opposite direction as if she couldn't care less whether we trashed the head teacher or not – it wasn't her problem.

"Well, I think it was kind of neat of him to see us off," I found myself saying.

Eve was looking at her watch. "Hadn't we better catch that train, Miss B?" she asked.

The librarian seemed not to hear. When she turned back to us, there was a sort of distant smile on her face. "Hm?"

"Ding-dong," said Lisa.

"We're all here, Miss B," I said. "We can go now."

"All right," said Miss Billingham. "Lead on then."

*

Lead on? It was only when we were on the train heading towards Ipswich that I was able to work out what was bothering me about Miss Billingham.

I was seated across the aisle with Roberta, Lisa and Charlie, who were looking at some teen magazine full of boys showing off their pecs and fake tans. Ellie and Eve were with Miss Billingham, and Tara had left us to roam the train with a dangerous look in her eyes.

Pretending to read a magazine I watched Miss Billingham as she gazed out of the window at the sights of east London flashing by – the houses, the factories, the parks and football pitches. After a while, she reached into her bag and took out a book. She ran her fingers over the front of the book, then, with a little sigh, opened it and started to read.

Eve asked her what she was reading.

"*Sense and Sensibility.*" There was kind of a warmth in Miss Billingham's voice I hadn't heard before. "I read it once a year. So romantic. Have you read Jane?"

"Er, no." Eve was glancing back down at her book with a little what-have-I-started? frown.

"What about you, Stevie? Have you been introduced to Jane Austen?" She tapped the front of the book which featured an old-fashioned couple looking kind of mournful.

"No, we haven't met. But I saw her movie."

Miss Billingham smiled as she returned to her reading. "You've got a treat awaiting you," she said. "A real treat."

It occurred to me briefly that maybe it hadn't been such a brilliant idea to invite someone who lived through books to take the Hotshots to a tournament. At school, she was so pale and quiet, her clothes so grey and brown that sometimes it was as if she wasn't a real person at all but was a character who had escaped from one of those old books of hers. Even at this early stage, she wasn't exactly coming on like Ms Authority Figure. Lead on, she had said, as if we were in charge of her, rather than the other way round.

"Hi, Mummy. Have you heard from Barry yet?" Meanwhile, Lisa had found another emergency call to make from her mobile. "Yeah, we caught the train all right and what – a film? That's brilliant!"

As soon as she had grabbed the attention of everyone in the carriage, Lisa moved into her favourite name-dropping routine. "Was Hugh there – Hugh Grant – and Michael Hutchence? Oh, wow, Mum."

Eventually she hung up, closing the phone with a showy little click. She opened her magazine, then, after a few seconds, looked up. "What?" she said. "Why are you all staring at me?"

Roberta (who's always the first to be taken in by this) asked as casually as she could manage what all that stuff about the stars was.

"Nothing." Lisa gave her hair a little showbiz shake.

"Come on, Lisa," said Charlie. "All that stuff about Hugh Grant and Michael Hutchence."

"Honestly, you guys." Lisa gave an impatient little sigh. "You're just so nosy." She waited a couple of beats, then muttered, as if she really didn't want to talk about it. "It's just my mum's up for this film part. She met a few of these guys at some audition party. It's no big deal."

"Big step up from the catfood ads," said some small-minded person. (All right, it was me.)

Lisa's eyes flashed dangerously.

20

"Let's not compare parents, shall we, Stevie. At least my mum's not like a total business zombie – unlike some parents we could mention." She stood up. "Anyone fancy a wander? I need some fresh air." She pushed past me. Moments later, Charlie, Roberta and Ellie followed her.

I caught Eve's eye. "Pathetic," she muttered. We both glanced at Miss Billingham.

She was still reading. For the first time I noticed the red scarf around her neck, the shiny new high-heeled shoes she wore on her feet.

"How's Jane?" I asked.

She smiled. "Wonderful," she said.

I wasn't in the mood for reading. For five minutes, I leafed through Roberta's magazine. Then, telling Miss Billingham and Eve that I was getting a soda, I set off to find the others.

They weren't hard to find. I just followed the noise. At the far end of the restaurant car, five of them sat, laughing and chatting, earning themselves heavy, disapproving looks from some of the other passengers who seemed to belong to the girls-should-shut-up-and-be-nice school of opinion.

"Where's Tara?" I put my Coke on the table and squeezed in beside Roberta.

"She said she had met some boys but they had gone by the time we arrived," said Lisa casually.

"And?"

"She got all moody for some reason." Lisa looked away.

There was a brief, embarrassed silence. "Why do I get the impression that I'm only hearing half the story?" I said.

"OK, so I made a joke about her frightening the boys off," said Lisa with a what-the-heck shrug. "She decided to take it the wrong way."

"Er, excuse me," said Ellie. "Your exact words were 'one look at you and they probably jumped off the train'."

"Charming," murmured Roberta.

"It was a joke," said Lisa, looking almost sorry. "She's been in a really weird mood since we left London."

"I don't think she's ever been away from home before," said Ellie.

"Sheesh, you guys." I stood up. "I thought we were meant to be a team."

Tara wasn't hard to find. She was standing at the door between the refreshment car and the next carriage. The window in front of her was wide open and she was staring out as the landscape of houses gave away to green fields. A cigarette was dangling from her right hand.

"How ya goin'?" I said.

She said nothing but took a long drag on her cigarette, then put her face out of the window to blow the smoke into the train's slipstream.

"Death wish, huh?" I tried a joke. "If the cigs don't get you, a bridge will knock your head off."

Tara's reply was a string of swear words.

"That Lisa," I said, trying to defuse the tension with a bit of friendly chat. "Talk about ego. Just because my parents said they'd lend me their mobile, she had to—"

"Cows!"

"What?"

"Look! Cows. In a field."

"Yeah." I smiled. "What a surprise."

22

"If there are cows where we're going, I'm out of there, man. I'm not being charged by a herd of bloomin' cows, no way." She did her cigarette routine again.

"Since when have you smoked?"

Tara turned to me for the first time. Perhaps it was because of the wind that had been blowing in her face but her eyes seemed unusually red. "Since when have you poked your nose into other people's business?"

I raised my hands in defeat. If Tara was into nicotine addiction, I guessed that was up to her.

"I hate the countryside," she said suddenly. "It's lame."

"D'you get out of town much?" I asked.

"Nah. Don't believe in the countryside." She glanced out of the window. "My dad says it's boring."

"It'll be all right. We'll have a good time."

"As long as there ain't no cows."

"Come on back, Tar. I'll buy you a Coke."

Tara threw her cigarette butt out of the window and, without another word, she followed me back to join the others.

It was a weird journey. By the time the train began to slow for Oakmere, we were back in the carriage, Miss Billingham had put Jane away, and even Tara had quietened down.

I was beginning to discover that, once you took the Hotshots away from their background – away from Broadhurst, away from their families – they seemed to become different people. It was as if, when we were at school, we were somehow part of some unit which we all kind of

23

understood. Away from it all, with only a dreamy librarian for company, we were each alone, individuals.

But no one was more different from her old self than Miss Billingham was. For the past few miles, she had been staring out of the window, at the woods, the meadows, the fields of corn being harvested. Occasionally she turned back to us and I could swear that her cheeks and neck seemed somehow to have reflected the colours that were outside. The smile that never seemed far from her lips was like that on the face of the woman on the front of her novel – kind of mysterious and secretive and inward.

For the life of me, I couldn't figure out why Miss Billingham, of all people, should have been happy to give up her holiday to take a football team of second-year girls to East Anglia. For the first time, it occurred to me that, to use one of my father's favourite phrases, she might have a hidden agenda.

"Where exactly is it we're staying?" Eve looked up from her book to ask.

"Ah, yes." Miss Billingham reached into her big sensible, leather shoulder-bag. "Cholmondley Manor. Mr Morley gave me a letter from Mrs Fairbrother."

She opened the letter and read the typewritten sheet.

"Our host is called Mrs Pritchard," she said. "And apparently her house is quite old and has lots of rooms."

"Uh-oh, sounds spooky," said Roberta.

"Does it say anything about cows?" asked Tara.

" 'My mother is looking forward to having some young company'," Miss Billingham read from the letter. "She's apparently a bit idiosyncratic—"

"What does that mean?" asked Tara.

"Mad," said Lisa, looking bored. "OK, so we're staying with a nutter."

"No, idiosyncratic simply means that she does things her own way," said Miss Billingham. "The letter goes on to say that we should make ourselves thoroughly at home and . . ." she paused, frowning, "not worry too much about Mrs Pritchard's odd little ways."

"Oh, wonderful," said Lisa. "That's going to be a great preparation for a tournament. Staying with a mad old pensioner who has odd little ways."

The train was slowing down. "Oakmere, we are approaching Oakmere," said a voice on the intercom.

"Too late now," said Charlie, standing and pulling her bag down from the luggage rack.

The train pulled into a tiny station which was like something out of an old film. We bundled out and made our way towards the exit as the train drew out. Moments later, we were standing on the steps of the station.

Alone.

"Like, dig the welcome," I muttered.

There were two cars, one very old and the other small and rusty, parked about fifty yards away.

A large man in his late thirties ambled, hands in pockets, towards us. There was something odd and old-fashioned about him – maybe it was his shaggy haircut, which made him look like an ageing pop star who's trying to be hip and not quite making it.

"Billingham," he called out.

"Miss Billingham, yes," said Miss Billingham.

"'Op in." He turned back to the car. "The name's Jim Walker. I work for Mrs Pritchard."

Nervously, we made our way to the two cars and put our bags in the trunk of the big old grey thing.

"Three of you can go with my missus," he nodded in the direction of the second car in which a woman with dirty-blond hair sat, drumming her fingers on the steering wheel in time to loud music from the car radio. Occasionally she drew on a cigarette and smoke billowed into the car.

After a discreet scramble for the bigger of the two cars, Roberta, Eve and I were left out.

"See you there," Ellie called out.

"If we don't die of passive smoking on the way," muttered Roberta.

I led the way to the second car, tried a smile on the woman which I guess must have bounced off the windscreen because she ignored it. I opened the back door to step into the car's deafening, smoky interior.

"Hi," I said.

The woman grunted, opened the window and chucked her cigarette butt onto the road as the car driven by her husband pulled away. Eve and Roberta squeezed in beside me, neither of them – hey, surprise – being particularly keen to sit in the front passenger seat.

"Is it far?" asked Eve in her best trying-to-be-polite voice.

"Far enough," said the woman, turning the radio up slightly.

Beside me, Roberta gave an eloquent little moan. "I wanna go home," she murmured through gritted teeth.

CHAPTER FOUR

Servants' Quarters

"Bumpy, eh?"

"Yeah."

These words, between Eve and our moody driver, were the sum total of the conversation on the way from the station to the house.

After about a five-mile drive, we had turned into a gateway and were bouncing our way down a long, pot-holed lane past a cottage, a couple of fields, then a wood. Cholmondley Manor, we were beginning to discover, was not exactly the kind of place where you could look over the fence to chat to neighbours.

We came over a hill and there was the house. Nestling in the valley, it blended so comfortably with the landscape that, with its ripe red bricks, tall, rickety chimneys, its dark windows with ditsy little diamond-shaped panes, it seemed as natural as if it had grown out of the earth itself.

"Wow," whispered Eve.

The two cars came to a halt in a courtyard, surrounded by farm buildings, at the back of the house. We got out and stared around us like tourists.

"Beautiful," whispered Miss Billingham. "It's like Manderley in *Rebecca*."

The driver of the big car was unloading our bags from the trunk. He nodded in the direction of a low back door that was open. "You'll find the old girl indoors," he said. Without another word, he stepped back into the car and drove off, followed by his wife.

"What a charming couple," said Roberta.

We picked up our bags and walked nervously towards the door.

"Anybody there?" Miss Billingham called into the dark interior. The only reply was the distant sound of a dog barking.

As we stood there, a duck appeared at the door, looked up at us, then waddled into the courtyard.

"OK, guys, you can wake me up now." Lisa shook her head. "I've had enough of this dream."

"A duck to greet us," muttered Roberta. "That quacks me up."

We walked into the house and found ourselves in a small, stone-floored hall, full of old boots and coats. There was a definite muddy, farmyard smell in the air. The dog's yapping could be heard more clearly now and something lower and croakier which might or might not have been a human voice. In spite of the heat outside, I shivered.

"Let's go to a hotel," said Tara. "There must be a town around here."

"Don't be daft, Tara. We're going to have a lovely time." Miss Billingham squared her shoulders and walked through the hall into the darkness of the house. "Helloo," she called out, a slight tremor in her voice. "We're here."

The barking grew louder.

"I'm in the kitchen." A voice, which sounded about a million years old, echoed down the corridors of the house.

We followed Miss Billingham through a big old dining room with loads of portraits of historical people on the wall, down another little passage.

"Come on." The croaky voice was showing signs of impatience. "Where are you?"

At the end of the corridor, we arrived at a huge, dusty kitchen with ancient brass pots hanging on the wall. Crouching on the floor, turned away from us, was a figure with curly grey hair wearing a kind of stained green jacket.

"Sorry not to greet you." The voice was deep, almost man-like. "Had to sort this old thing out."

We gathered around. The woman held a grey chicken on her knee. In her right hand was a kitchen knife. It was a scene out of a vegetarian's nightmare.

"Won't take a second," the old woman was muttering. "Just a quick cut will do the trick."

"No!" The agonized squeak came from Ellie. "No, please don't do that."

"Mm?"

For the first time, the old woman looked up at us. Caught in the evening sunlight that was pouring through the murky kitchen window, her face seemed ancient beyond belief, the skin hanging in wrinkled folds like sheets on an unmade bed, her chin tumbling downwards in crazy snowdrifts of soft flesh until it became her neck. Over her top lip, there was a small, dark moustache.

"Please don't kill that hen," said Ellie bravely. "It . . ."

For a moment she hesitated. "It hasn't done you any harm, has it?"

A weird, wheezing sound came from the woman as, with much creaking, she stood up, and held the chicken with both hands.

"I'm not cutting her throat, you clot," she said to Ellie. "I'm just cleaning her up a bit. Want to help?" Without waiting for a reply, she thrust the chicken into Ellie's hands, then started rummaging between its legs. "Bloody awful case of diarrhoea," she said casually. "Just need to cut out a few of these tail feathers."

"Diarrhoea?" Ellie swallowed hard but held on to the chicken. "Right. Fine."

"Oh, please. Puke in a box," said Roberta, stepping back.

Miss Billingham cleared her throat nervously. "It's been a bit of a long journey, actually," she said. "Is there any chance of seeing our rooms?"

The old woman glanced at her. "Right-oh," she said, taking the hen from Ellie and putting it on the floor where, with obvious relief, it hurried out of the kitchen. "I'll do that later."

She threw the knife onto the kitchen table, then held out a bony hand. "Daphne Pritchard," she said.

With a sort of wince, Miss Billingham shook hands. "Pleased to meet you," she said. "I'm Diana Billingham and these are the Hotshots." As she introduced us one by one, she wiped her palm down the side of her dress.

"I can only remember animals' names," said Mrs Pritchard in an absent-minded way. "Let's have some tea, then you can find your rooms. I bought a cake from the village shop." She opened a big, square tin and reached for the knife she had just put down.

"Er, maybe not that one," Roberta said quickly.

"Mm?" The old woman frowned as she stared at the knife, then gave a bark of laughter. "Quite right, well spotted, that girl," she said opening a drawer and taking out another knife.

She turned and stopped, staring at us as if she had just noticed we were there. "You're very old," she said.

We glanced at one another. Like, *we* were old?

"Mary said you were just little girls who wanted a few days in the country." Mrs Pritchard shook her head, frowning.

"No, we're big," said Lisa. "We're here to play football."

"Not like Mary to to be thinking about other people, but she insisted," she muttered. "These little girls need a holiday in the country. What was that about football?"

As she cut the cake, we stared at one another, lost for words.

Something very, very weird was going on here.

After tea in the dining room, which featured the driest cake in the history of all cakes, we discovered another small item of bad news. After Miss Billingham had floated off to the guest bedroom where she would be staying, we made our way to the top of the house where Mrs Pritchard had told us we would be sleeping, in the servants' quarters. ("Servants? Charming," Roberta had muttered.)

Within ten seconds, two rooms had gone – the first to Charlie and Roberta, the second to Ellie and Eve.

Lisa glanced from me to Tara as we stood in the narrow corridor. "Looks like it's us three together in the big room," she said with a definite lack of enthusiasm.

"Shut up us three." Tara's eyes flashed angrily. "No way am I sleeping in the same room as you two. You'll be yakking all night."

"I'm not exactly thrilled by the idea of waking up to see your ugly mush either," said Lisa.

As Tara stepped forward, I moved between them.

"Hey guys, hullo, anyone care about little old me here?" I said quickly. "Am I like Miss Invisible all of a sudden?"

"I wish—" muttered Lisa.

"How about you having the big room with Eve and Ellie?" I gave Lisa the benefit of an icily insincere smile. "That way you won't have to put up with Tara or me."

Lisa shrugged, then wandered into one of the smaller bedrooms where Eve and Ellie were sitting. "I've got us the big room," she said moodily.

Kind of pleased with this small diplomatic achievement, I wandered into the first room with Tara, shut the door behind us and slumped onto one of the beds.

Tara opened her bag, spilling some clothes on to the floor, and took out a plastic football. She opened a wardrobe and kicked the ball against the cupboard, rhythmically, again and again, her face closed up with sullen misery.

Sighing, I opened a magazine and pretended to read.

"This is the lamest house," Tara said eventually. "The granny's well mental, there's a duck in the hall, a chicken with diarrhoea's running around the kichen and there's probably a ghost in every room."

"I'm sure we'll be fine," I murmured unconvincingly and returned to my magazine.

Moments later, there were raised voices from the next-door room.

Sheesh, now what? Followed by Tara, I went to see what was going on.

"Problem." Eve was looking accusingly at Lisa. "I went downstairs to ask Mrs Pritchard if I could use her phone to tell my parents we've arrived safely. It's out of order."

"Yeah? So we'll have to use Lisa's mobile." I shrugged.

"Tell them, Lisa," said Eve.

Lisa was lying on her bed, eyes closed. "It doesn't work," she said.

"How d'you mean it doesn't work? You've been chatting away all day on it."

"Try it if you like."

I picked up the mobile and switched it on. It was dead.

"How could it be working one minute and not now?" asked Charlie.

"Search me," said Lisa.

There was something oddly defensive about her. Then, suddenly, I saw it all. "It never did work, did it?" I said.

Lisa shrugged.

"If it didn't work, who was she making those calls to?" asked Eve.

"Herself," I said. "That's right, isn't it, Lisa?"

Lisa pouted. "Mum didn't pay the bill," she muttered. "I was kind of playing a joke on you all."

"Hilarious," said Roberta.

Normally, we might have laughed about Lisa's supersad

deception but now a gloomy silence descended on the room like a cold mist as the reality of our situation seeped through to each of us.

We were in an old house miles away from anywhere. The person we were staying with had no idea why we were there. And we couldn't phone our parents.

Great start.

CHAPTER FIVE

Dorks on the Wall

"Golly, gals, look at us!"

It was the next morning. The sun was shining, a big dinosaur-like machine was cutting corn in a field, birds were singing everywhere, and we were on our way down the drive from Cholmondley Manor to catch a bus to Oakmere.

"I said, golly gals, look at us!" Oh yeah, and Lisa had bounced back from last night's humiliation as only Lisa can. She skipped ahead of us, pretending to be a cute little seven-year-old. "We're all having a spiffing good time in the jolly old country, eh what?" she called out. "Just like the Famous Seven."

"Famous Seven? I don't think so," said Roberta.

"Five," said Ellie. "Either the Famous Five or the Secret Seven."

"Would someone mind telling me what you're talking about?" I said.

"It's Enid Blyton." Miss Billingham smiled as she followed us. To our general amazement, she had appeared this morning wearing jeans and a jazzy plaid shirt and was looking almost relaxed. "She was an English author who wrote stories about chums who go for picnics in the countryside and have lashings of ginger beer."

"Wasn't one of them called Titty?" said Roberta. When we all laughed, she said, "No, seriously, there was a girl called Titty."

"Actually, that was *Swallows and Amazons* by Arthur Ransome," said Eve.

"I would so hate to be called Titty," said Ellie.

"Not much danger of that," said Roberta under her breath.

We reached the end of the drive. In a cottage by the gate, Jim Walker was digging in his front garden.

"Morning," Miss Billingham called out.

Walker stopped digging and stared at us moodily. "How do," he said, following us with his eyes until we reached the gate.

"Gosh, we're all frightfully friendly round here," Lisa sang out, still in Enid Blyton mode.

As we stood at the bus stop, which was a few yards from the gate, I thought back to early that morning when we had seen Mrs Walker down at the manor. Mrs Pritchard had said she came in twice a week to clean but, as far as I could see, the job involved little more than making a lot of noise, banging an old vacuum cleaner into the furniture and making everyone feel kind of embarrassed.

After about five minutes, a green single-decker bus trundled around the corner and pulled up.

"Morning, girls." The driver, a young crew-cutted guy, greeted us with a cheeky smile, as we queued to buy our tickets. "Going shopping, are we?"

There was a little tremor of irritation among us.

"Actually," Lisa said in her iciest tones, "we're playing football."

For some reason, the bus driver seemed to find this the funniest thing he had heard all day – that was until Tara stepped on the bus. She looked down at the driver, bouncing her football as he waited for her fare. "Got a problem with that, have you, mate?"

The driver shrugged, his oafish sexist smile fading quickly. "No problem, love," he said.

Here was the deal: Oakmere FC, who were running the tournament, had suggested we might like a training session on the pitch where our matches would be played.

Although none of us, with the possible exception of Tara, was feeling exactly football-minded (the sun was hot, we hadn't played a match for months, there was no Gerry Phelan to coach us), we had agreed to show up. Hey, what harm could a kickabout do?

But, when we arrived at the ground which was on the outskirts of the town (that is, about half a mile from its centre), it quickly became clear that around these parts they took their soccer kind of seriously.

A wiry athletic-looking little guy in a tracksuit greeted us in front of the clubhouse. Behind him, we could see, at one end of the eleven-a-side pitch, a team of teenage boys doing sprinting practice. Now and then the enraged screams of their manager drifted across to us.

"Gibson's the name." Our host shook hands with Miss Billingham, then smiled at us. "Ready for the tournament?"

"Er, no." The voice of Roberta carried from the back of the group.

Mr Gibson raised an eyebrow, as if to say that football was not a joking matter. He turned back to Miss Billingham. "Would you be looking for a training match? Fitness routines?"

"Well . . ." Miss Billingham glanced helplessly in my direction.

"Maybe some work on set pieces?"

"We just want a kick-around." I spoke up quickly before Miss Billingham destroyed what little reputation the Hotshots had in these parts by quoting Jane Austen on the sweeper system or something. "We sort of coach ourselves."

"Yeah?" Gibson gave a well-I'll-be-darned double-take. "OK, please yourselves." He pointed to the pitch. "That's your half," he said. "Maybe you'd like a practice game against the boys later."

"What?" It was Eve who allowed her alarm to show.

"Only kidding." Gibson gave what he probably thought was a humorous wink.

"Sheesh," said Roberta. "How come everyone's a sexist around here? Is it something they put in the water?"

That football practice was not exactly our most glorious hour. Some of us (take a bow, Lisa Martin) had other things on our minds than football. Others (thank you, Tara Williams) seemed to have been fazed by the realities of country life. And then there was no coach – no Gerry

Phelan – to shake us out of this weird mood we all found ourselves in.

Another problem. To our surprise, the visit from a girls' football team from London seemed like some sort of big deal around here. So it wasn't just the Hotshots goofing off and making fools of themselves on that practice pitch. It was total public humiliation.

A few yards from where the goals had been set up was a low wall. There, the local heavy mob – some boys a couple of years older than us and a couple of manky-looking girls, all T-shirts and greasy hair and torn jeans – were perched, chewing, smoking, laughing, drumming their heels on the wall, waiting for the show to begin.

We did some passing practice. They trilled sarcastically every time we touched the ball.

We took shots at Tara in goal. They jeered every time we missed.

We had a brief practice game. They chanted, "Boring, boring Hotshots", and "What a load of rubbish." I swear these people made Jason and his crew from school look like cool sophisticates.

We grew hot and flustered. Normally, when this kind of thing happened back home, a few choice words from Tara and Charlie would help remind people that the Hotshots didn't always play by nice-girl rules, but both of them were keeping grimly silent.

Occasionally, I glanced at Miss Billingham, who was watching us from the other side of the pitch, but she too had chosen to ignore the dorks on the wall.

After half an hour, during which what little confidence we had just like drained away, we packed up and, with the sound of jeering in our ears, made our way back to Miss Billingham.

"All right?" She smiled brightly. "Satisfactory practice?"

"Nope," said Lisa.

"It didn't exactly help having a bunch of local dweebs laughing at us." Roberta spoke with quiet fury.

"They were just bored," said Miss Billingham. "There's nothing you can do about that sort of thing."

"Surely, if we're the guests here, we deserve a bit of politeness." Eve's thin lips quivered with disapproval. "Couldn't you have said something to the bloke in the tracksuit?"

"Me? Why on earth should I do that?"

It took a couple of moments for us all to take in what Miss Billingham had said.

"Because, like, hullo, ding-dong . . ." I tried to choose my words carefully, remembering that Miss B was one sensitive item. "Because you're meant to be in charge, aren't you?"

"I agreed to accompany seven girls on a trip to the countryside," said Miss Billingham quietly. "No more, no less. I'm a librarian, not a teacher. Being 'in charge' is not what I'm here for."

"Oh, great," said Lisa.

"So you're just going to have to sort out your problems yourselves." Miss Billingham glanced at her watch. "Now, I have a call to make. Would you like to meet up at the bus stop in one hour's time?"

"Sure," muttered Roberta, adding under her breath, "if that's not too organized for you."

*

"An hour to kill in Oakmere," said Lisa, after Miss Billingham had left. "Just how are we going to pack it all in?"

"I want to look into that really interesting little museum we saw in the town centre," said Eve in her best frightfully jolly voice. "Anyone coming?"

"Eve." Lisa put her hand on Eve's shoulder. "You don't have to do this. Your parents aren't here. No one's looking. Relax."

"I am relaxed, thank you very much, Lisa. There's an exhibition about old-fashioned ways of farming. I happen to find it rather interesting."

"I'm up for that," said Ellie, picking up her bag. "Maybe it'll give me ideas for my organic farming project."

"Well, I'm going to ring my mum," said Roberta. "Shall we go?"

We were just moving off towards the High Street when we noticed that Tara was holding back.

"I'm staying here," she said. "I'm a bit tired."

"Tired?" We all spoke at once.

"Yeah, why not?" Tara sat down on the grass and leant on her kitbag. "I'm beyond tired."

"She had a bad night." I spoke quietly, not wanting to provoke one of Tara's rages. The fact was, I had woken several times during the night to find my room-mate staring out of the window or pacing the room. Once she seemed to be sitting up in bed, staring into the darkness, holding her football to her as if it were a teddy bear. It was fair to say that Tara was taking a bit of time to get used to life in the country.

"Bog off and leave me alone." She lay down, her head

on her kitbag, and closed her eyes. "I'll see you at the bus stop."

So we did the sights of Oakmere. The breathtaking Boots the Chemist! The unforgettable WH Smith and Sons! That shimmering glory in the late afternoon, FW Woolworths! Forget, "See Naples and die" – it was, like, "See Oakmere and then have a nice cup of tea."

But here's a funny thing. Although there was nothing much to see, we laughed and relaxed. We found a call box and took turns at calling our parents. We walked up and down the pedestrian High Street without being jostled or shouted at or followed by weirdos. Compared to people back home, the shoppers here seemed at ease with one another. In the city, when four girls are making a bit of noise and cracking up with laughter, there tends to be dirty looks and general, wall-to-wall disapproval. Here they smiled at you and pretty soon you started smiling back.

OK, so we were laughing at this Hicksville, with its sad fashion boutiques and record shops with about five of the latest releases, but I guess each of us, in our own way, was thinking, so what if it's kind of ditsy and old-fashioned? Maybe it's not so terrible to be a touch out of date if it means you can worry a bit less about being up-to-the-minute, on-the-button, attitude-conscious and all those other hyphenated crazinesses.

I say each of us. It would be fair to say that Lisa was not totally impressed by the sights of Oakmere. She didn't believe the fashion items in the shop windows. How did these people accessorize? Er, whatever happened to the twentieth century?

Yet even she seemed happy as we made our way slowly

back to the bus stop – what she said was negative but the look on her face was telling a different story. No, I think old Lisa was coming to terms with life in the country, no problem.

There were only two things that were spoiling my generally good mood. One was the thought of the tournament ahead of us. The Hotshots had never just been a bunch of girls kicking a football about: we were winners. Yet, right now, none of us had got our heads around the idea of the match ahead of us. Somehow, losing – losing badly, even – would strike at what was special between us.

It occurred to me, for the first time, that maybe the Hotshots were in danger of splitting up, and that, if we weren't thinking of ourselves as a team, then what was there left? Bottom line, none of us had that much in common with each other – it was football that kept us together. Without it, we would be on our own.

Talking of which, there was my other worry.

"I think I'll just go and check that Tara hasn't fallen asleep."

The three of them looked at me without exactly bothering to hide their surprise. "What are you on, Stevie?" asked Lisa. "Ever since we've been here, you've been all concerned and serious."

"I just don't want Tara to miss the bus, OK?"

Seething, I turned to make my way up the High Street. Fact is, the trip to Oakmere had been basically down to me – if someone was having a bad time, I couldn't just walk away from her.

Even if her name was Tara Williams.

Deep in thought, I reached the football ground. At one

43

end of the pitch, a team was still practising. At the other, the rough boys were still hanging around the wall. There was no sign of Tara.

How could I have mistrusted her? I turned back towards the town. Even Tara was able to get to a bus stop by a particular time, right?

Wrong.

A long, low whistle echoed around the ground behind my back. I knew that whistle.

I looked back. One of the boys on the wall seemed to be waving at me. I turned and walked a few paces. It wasn't one of the boys. It was Tara. My heart thumping, I made my way towards them.

Bottom line, I was scared. There were six of them – four boys, two girls – and Tara. As they sat there, smiling at me, drumming the heels of their boots on the wall, I felt kind of out of place.

It was like Barbie meets the Wild Bunch.

"Yo." A cigarette dangled from Tara's right hand. For the first time since we had left London, she was the old Tara I knew – and, right then, I wished she wasn't. "How's it goin', Stevie?"

"The others are at the bus stop," I said. "I thought I'd check out where you were."

"Well, I do declare she's an American." The oldest and biggest of the boys grinned at me from under a heavy overhang of dark greasy hair.

Ignoring him, I said, "I was kind of worried, Tara."

The two girls set up a cat's chorus, imitating my voice. "Kaanda werrried," was their version. The boys laughed and banged the palms of their hands on the wall, as if it was the best impression they had ever heard.

"Hilarious," I said quietly. "You coming?" I asked Tara.

"Where you stayin'?" The guy with the heavy black hair stared at me but Tara answered.

"Chummy Manor or something." She inhaled on her cigarette and coughed. "There's this mad granny there, with all these weird old pictures and animals wandering in and out of the house. We call her the Pilchard. Talk about mournful, man. It's beyond."

I didn't like Tara talking about Mrs Pritchard that way and telling these guys where we were staying didn't seem the most brilliant idea either, but it was too late now.

The dark-haired boy jumped down from the wall. "We got a couple of cutters – we'll take you there."

"Cutters?" I asked, thinking, so is this how they get around in Oakmere – on mowing-machines?

"Bikes." Haircut was standing in front of me, looking down in a way that made me feel uncomfortable. "Motor . . . bikes," he said as if I was some kind of lamebrain.

"Yessss." Tara jumped down from the wall. "Show me to 'em."

"You go with Dave." The boy seemed to have lost interest in Tara and was standing so close to me that I was getting a barfsome whiff of his dirty T-shirt. "I'll take little Yankee Doodle here." He winked and nodded in the direction of an enormous motorbike. "Climb on, babe."

"I haven't got a helmet and I'm not your—"

"Toni." Without looking back, he held out his hand in

the direction of the two girls on the wall. "Lend us your helmet."

The girl shrugged and passed him a helmet.

"No." I backed away, ready to run if I had to. "They're waiting for us at the bus stop. We don't know the way to the house." I gave Tara one last chance. "Coming?"

To my surprise, Tara slithered off the wall and slouched towards me. "See you, Bigstuff." She brushed past my greasy friend, throwing her cigarette butt on the ground. "Tomorrow maybe."

"How about Miss America?" The lead biker tried what he obviously thought was a sexy smile, revealing a row of front teeth like a road crash.

"Sounds good." I smiled, adding quietly as I turned away, "Like, when hell freezes over, right."

Tara walked beside me, swaggering as if she was wearing leathers and heavy boots.

"Bigstuff?" I said. "He calls himself *Bigstuff*? Is he serious?"

"Good name," said Tara.

"As if."

"I wanna ride on them cutters. I'm through with that mad Pilchard and her stupid animals."

I was just about to reply when I saw something which made me forget about Tara and the Oakmere boys with their cutters.

In an old-fashioned red telephone box just off the High Street, a woman was talking on the telephone. Something about the way she stood, cradling the phone as if it was a baby, almost crouched over, suggested that the conversation she was having was kind of intimate and intense.

46

"Is that . . .?" Tara had seen the woman too. "It is. That's Miss B, isn't it?" Before I could stop her, she had walked up to the telephone box and had tapped on the glass.

Miss Billingham gave a little start, turned then looked at her watch. She spoke for another few seconds, then emerged from the telephone box.

"The others are at the—" I hesitated. There seemed to be the hint of a tear in the librarian's eyes, yet her face was just one big smile – the sort of smile that just won't shift even if you try to think of something really sad. "Are you all right, Miss B?"

"Me?" Miss Billingham gave a light, happy laugh. "I've never been better in my life," she said.

CHAPTER SIX

A Ghostly Prisoner

But then maybe Mrs Pritchard wasn't quite so normal. That evening as we tried to eat one of the truly barfsome meals in which she specialized, I began to worry a bit about our host.

The problem was simple: her world began and ended with animals. So, for example, talking to us over dinner was no more than an interruption of the really important conversation, which was with her soulmate, the evil little dark Pekinese dog she called Bournville – an animal that was not only yappy, charmless, old and blind but, we discovered that night, had other medical problems.

Mrs Pritchard and Ellie were having one of their really interesting conversations – Mrs P trying to convert Ellie to the joys of shooting birds and chasing foxes with dogs and Ellie explaining the joys of vegetarianism (I mean, why bother, right?) – when we all became aware of, shall we say, a major gas attack.

"Pooh, d'you have to?" Lisa said to Roberta. "That is so disgusting."

"Charming," said Roberta. "It wasn't me – it must be Eve."

"What are you a—?" As the deadly smell reached Eve, she started coughing. "Oh no."

Soon we were all laughing and gasping for air, except for Ellie who was mid-sermon and, as usual, had noticed nothing.

Mrs Pritchard glanced around the table, then sniffed the air as if some rather pleasant fragrance had drifted in from the garden. "Oh Bournville!" she chortled, causing her tumble of chins to wobble. "What a revolting smell!"

"He's been doing it all meal," said Lisa. "Maybe he should wait outside."

"I've never heard anything so ridiculous. The poor old dog's got a chill and an upset tummy, that's all. I wish I knew what to give him."

"A cork, maybe," murmured Roberta.

"He seems to be having difficulty breathing." Ellie leant down to stroke the Pekinese's head. "Maybe we should get him some Vick to inhale – that's what my mum makes me do when I've got a chill."

"Excellent idea, what a clever girl." Mrs Pritchard dabbed at her mouth with one of the stained rags which were meant to be napkins. "We'll do that after supper."

Picture the scene. Ellie and Mrs Pritchard are on the ground in the sitting room, one on each side of a black Pekinese. It has a teacloth over its head which is being held over a saucepan steaming with Vick. Now and then Bournville gives a complaining moan.

"I've seen it all now," said Lisa, as the rest of us watched.

"No way will that thing work on a dog," said Tara.

"At least it's slowed down the action at the other end," laughed Roberta. "Maybe he needed a bit of a shock."

Mrs Pritchard was gazing at an old table near by. "I'm sure there was a china hare on that table," she muttered as if to herself. "Where could Jill have put it? It's one of my favourites."

"We could look for it tomorrow," said Mrs Pritchard's new best friend, Ellie.

"Whenever I ask Jill about my things, she gives me an awful look and tells me she's never seen it. Talks to me as if I've gone potty." For a moment, Mrs Pritchard looked frail and old. "Perhaps I have."

There was a brief silence.

"Any chance of a bit of telly?" Tara asked cheerfully.

Mrs Pritchard frowned. "Telly?"

"TV," said Lisa. "Like, the wireless with pictures?"

"I think there may be a set in the old billiard room," said Mrs Pritchard. "Only black and white, I'm afraid."

"Black and white?" Tara shook her head in disbelief. "This place gets weirder every day."

Tara, I noticed, was a bit more herself that evening. She no longer had that kind of spooked look of someone who thought something strange and scary – a cow, maybe – was waiting for her around every corner. I figured that maybe meeting Bigstuff and his pals had reminded her that, even in Oakmere, there were people around that she could relate to.

She slept well that night – and that was when I discovered

that Tara sleeping was every bit as much of a problem as Tara awake.

It was pitch black when I awoke the first time. A giant seemed to be dragging something heavy and rattling across the floor. After a few seconds, it dawned on me that this was what Tara sounded like when she was snoring.

"Tara." My voice seemed small and quiet in the darkness. "*Tara*." There was a snuffling noise from across the room, a few seconds of normal breathing – then the giant was back at work once more.

I lay in the darkness. Somewhere, in the distance, a church bell rang once. What seemed like about a million hours later, it rang again. Two o'clock. Bottom line, it wasn't just Tara's tonsils that were keeping me awake. Two evenings of the Pritchard diet were taking effect – my stomach ached with hunger. I decided to raid the kitchen.

I got out of bed and made my way to the door. It was dark in the corridor but, having been awake for hours, I was able to see my way through the gloom.

Down the stairs, holding tight on to the banister. Along the corridor where Miss Billingham's and Mrs Pritchard's rooms were. There were little taps and creaks and rustles from distant parts of the house, almost as if it had a life of its own. Past Miss B's room, then Mrs Pritchard's from where I could hear Bournville's snores, a wetter, less healthy version of Tara's night chorus.

Top of the main stairs. It seemed darker now. Only hunger propelled me down those wide stairs, towards the slow ticking grandfather clock in the hall. There was a brief metallic noise from the darkness downstairs, a strange sort of murmur.

Hey, imagination, Stevie. Think toast, think biscuits. Turn right at the bottom of the stairs and you'll be—

I froze where I stood, on the little landing a few steps up from the hall. The hairs on the back of my neck rose. My skin crawled with icy terror.

Because there, moving across the hall, from the sitting room to the study, was a dark human shape. It moved swiftly and silently as if no part of it was touching the ground. Backwards and forwards it went – three, four times – almost as if it was trapped and was trying to escape, as if, every night, it paced backwards and forwards, a ghostly prisoner at Cholmondley Manor.

A step backwards, then another, the sound of my heart pounding in my ear, my mouth dry, too terrified to scream. Back down the corridor. Up the stairs. Shut the door, now crying a little, my hands fumbling for a bolt, for a lock, for anything that would protect me from the presence downstairs.

In careful silence, I wedged a chair against the door, then scurried back to my bed.

Lie still. Maybe it won't see me. "Tara?"

But she was sleeping deeply, beyond snores, beyond terror.

Alone, I stared into the darkness, my ears straining for the creak on the stairs, too afraid to move.

Sleepless, alone, terrified, I did what my parents were always telling me to do every night but which I usually forgot.

I prayed.

CHAPTER SEVEN

Jitterbug

You stay awake all night. You listen to hour after hour of the loudest snores in the world. You are visited by a strange, ghostly presence. You experience what is almost certainly the worst twelve hours of your entire life. You expect a little sympathy, right?

Er, wrong. With the Hotshots of Broadhurst Comprehensive, it takes more than a major life-changing trauma to catch their attention.

Most of breakfast was the usual fight over cereal, sleepy chat, a minor skirmish between Roberta and Charlie as to who should do the washing-up. Ellie chatted away, Pilchard-style, to Bournville. Miss Billingham seemed in her own little world. Mrs Pritchard herself scuttled in and out of the dining room, looking more wacko than ever. "The silver," she was muttering to herself. "I'm sure we had more silver spoons than this."

It was only after several minutes that it was noticed that I was sitting, not saying a word, as I ate my cornflakes at the end of the table.

"What's up with you, Stevie Rostand?" asked Lisa chirpily.

Yeah, and thanks for the sympathy, Lisa. I continued eating in silence.

"She looks like she's seen a ghost," joked Charlie.

"I have."

"Shut up ghost," snapped Tara. "If you tell me there's a ghost in this old place, I'm outta here."

"I think I saw something last night."

Briefly, I had their attention. In a low voice, I told them what had happened.

"It was a dream," said Eve when I had finished. "I've had some really weird dreams here, too."

"As if it was a dream. I was as awake as I am now."

A slight chill of alarm had descended on the room.

"You've done it now," grumbled Tara. "You are beyond, Stevie."

"That's what it seemed like," I said. "Like something from . . . beyond."

Miss Billingham dabbed at her mouth with a napkin. "I'm sure there's a perfectly logical explanation," she said briskly. "Don't you agree, Mrs Pritchard?"

The old woman sat slightly apart from us. "What's that, dear?" she asked in a distracted voice.

"Stevie thinks she saw something last night."

"Something?"

"Or someone."

Mrs Pritchard frowned. "If there was anyone here, I'm sure I would have seen it," she said. "I get up quite often at night."

"There you are." Miss Billingham smiled with relief. "That's who you saw, Stevie. Mrs Pritchard."

I nodded. "Maybe." I glanced at Mrs Pritchard and, for

the briefest of moments, I caught an odd look – sort of sad and enquiring – in her eyes. Then she turned away.

Was she aware of something which she wasn't about to tell us? I thought back to that dark figure I had seen in the early hours of the morning. Unless the old lady moved at twice the speed that she did in the daytime at night, what I saw hadn't been her. I was sure that she knew it but, for some reason, she wasn't letting on.

My parents work at their bank like twenty-five hours every day. When they see their daughter ("Hullo, I'm Stevie Rostand – we met a few months back?"), they often have the pale, out-of-it look of people whose life is spent in front of a computer screen or at a meeting or on an aeroplane flying to another computer or to another meeting.

This means they're kind of protected from the real world. The first time Lisa came to dinner, they looked at her like she was some sort of extraterrestrial (all right, she did drink from the fingerbowl but, hey, no one's perfect). As for when they met Tara, it was plonk plonk, the sound of two chins hitting the ground.

"Strange days," is what my Daddy says on these occasions. "Strange days, strange ways."

That day at Cholmondley Manor, I knew what he meant. By ten o'clock the sun was beating down as if we were in some tropical country. Rather than risk another encounter with Bigstuff and his biking pals, the Hotshots had set up a couple of goals and were playing a practice game of two-touch on the lawn.

For some reason, it was our best training session for

months. Lisa rediscovered her confidence, and was playing the fancy little tricks and shimmies we thought she had forgotten. The old instinctive sense of where the other players on your team are going to be seemed to be returning even to Eve. Three against three, with a rolling substitute, we forgot all the worries and problems of our trip to the countryside as we rediscovered the joy of playing good, fast, passing football with friends.

I was substitute when Miss Billingham emerged from the house. As she stood beside me, watching the game in silence, I became aware of something weird and unusual – from the direction of Miss B, the quiet, grey, mousy librarian, came the unmistakable smell of perfume. This morning she smelt expensive, feminine, even (was I dreaming?) sexy. I glanced in her direction. She was wearing a pink silk blouse and there was even a hint of lipstick and make-up on her face.

She clapped her hands at the next break in play.

"I have to go to Oakmere to meet a friend," she announced with an odd, distant smile.

"A friend?" said Tara, showing her usual brand of tact. "In Oakmere?"

"Yes, I do have friends." Beneath the make-up, a hint of a blush became visible. "And one of them, by a happy coincidence, lives near here. If any of you want to go into town, stay together and make sure you're back by five o'clock this evening."

"But Miss B." A little frown of disapproval was on Eve's face. "The tournament's the day after tomorrow."

Miss Billingham laughed lightly in a way I'd never heard from her before. "Yes, Eve," she said. "So you'd better keep practising, hadn't you?" She turned and waved girl-ishly. "See you later, then."

After she had left, we stood looking after her for a few seconds.

"Well, I think that's rather irresponsible," said Eve.

"Maybe she's discovered an exciting new book in the library," said Roberta.

I shook my head. "Happy coincidence?" I said thoughtfully. "I don't think so."

It grew hotter. After the game, we sat on the lawn, drinking orange squash, watching Mrs Pritchard as she tended her roses. Despite the weather, she wore these heavy brown trousers. A floppy straw hat almost hid her face but as she worked we could hear her talking to Bournville, who was lying near by, panting in the shade of a yew tree.

"The Pilchard is actually kneeling on poo," Roberta said suddenly. "I'm sorry, but I call that seriously weird."

"It's manure." As usual, Ellie was the first to defend Mrs Pritchard.

"Manure, poo, same difference." Tara stabbed at the lawn with a stick she had found. "We're living with an old woman who shaves chickens' bums, kneels in poo and talks to a dog that farts all the time."

"She's no weirder than you are," said Ellie.

"I feel a bit sorry for her," said Eve. "All alone with only Mr and Mrs Psycho Walker looking after her."

"That woman's so rude to her," said Ellie. "This morning Mrs Pritchard asked her if she'd seen the silver. Mrs Walker spoke to her as if she was a loony. 'You haven't

57

had any silver for years,' she said in this really slow, insulting voice. 'You're getting confused,' she said."

I lay back on the grass and stared at the house. There was something strange about Cholmondley Manor, I had decided – not so much spooky as just . . . not quite right. Why should the Walkers be so hostile to the woman who was employing them? Why did Mrs Fairbrother suddenly decide to send us along? Why hadn't she told her mother anything about us? It was as if we were part of some weird game and no one had told us the rules.

"Hullo, ding-dong." Roberta was prodding me with her foot. "We're all going into Oakmere. You coming, Stevie?"

"Hm? I'm kind of pooped," I said. "I think I'll stay here and catch up on a bit of sleep."

They looked at me as if I had said something totally weird.

"What?" I said. "You all got a problem with that?"

"We were thinking of calling in at the Sports Centre." Lisa had that suit-yourself pout on her face. "We want to find out more about the tournament."

"And?" I was just beginning to get a hint of what was on their minds.

"And you're the person who set all this up, so you should do the talking, right?" snapped Lisa.

"What, you mean suddenly I'm captain? Hey, great."

They looked embarrassed.

"You know that I'm captain," said Lisa with an angry little shake of the head.

"But you don't want to do the talking – strange, that."

"I'm outta here," said Lisa, and the others prepared to go. "I don't know what it is but you have a severe attitude problem, Stevie. Remember you weren't even in the Hot-shots when we first started."

I looked away. If anyone had an attitude problem, it was Little Miss Ego herself, but pointing that out definitely fell into the life's-too-short category.

"You all right, Stevie?" Charlie asked.

"I'm fine," I said. "Just a bit tired."

"We're ringing Jamie to tell him how we're getting on," said Roberta. "Any messages?"

"Yeah," I said. "Tell him we need him out here with his ghostbusters kit."

I watched them as they made their way down the drive, chatting and laughing in the sun. It was a weird thing, but being away from Broadhurst, away from families, somehow made each of the Hotshots more of a person, less part of a team. Lisa's love affair with herself became the Real Thing. Ellie talked about nothing but animals. Eve disapproved of the rest of us even more than ever. Charlie was quiet and defensive. Roberta was unable to take anything seriously.

And where did Stevie Rostand fit in with all this? I turned back to the garden. When I had first joined the team, it had been like, Hello, notice me, I may be American and different from you guys but, hey, I can shout as loud as any of you. You want flash, you want ego? Get a load of this.

But recently I had found myself making less noise while organizing quietly behind the scenes.

My daddy's favourite pearl of wisdom, "Bottom line, bub – it's dog-eat-dog out there. You gotta look after number one."

It was a me-first world my parents belonged to, all sharp elbows and in-your-face aggression. Sure, I wanted to be like them but, since I joined the Hotshots, I had begun to think that the best way to look after number one was to see that numbers two, three, four, five and the rest were rubbing along OK. It was weird – I mean, I had actually found myself worrying about the demon snorer Tara.

What was happening to me? It was as if I was becoming a teacher or something.

"These roses are almost as old as me."

I found I was standing behind Mrs Pritchard in her manure patch. Somehow, without turning around, she had been aware of my presence.

"They're beautiful," I said.

She glanced up at me. "Not going to Oakmere?"

"I didn't sleep last night. I was gonna hit the sack for a while."

"Hit the sack." The old woman chuckled to herself. "You Americans do make me laugh."

"Yeah?" I said coldly.

"I knew some Americans in the war." Mrs Pritchard sat back on her haunches and stared ahead as if I wasn't there. "They were such fun. Made the English boys look so . . . stuffy. We used to dance something called the jitterbug. I wonder where they are now."

I hesitated. It didn't seem right to point out that, fifty years on, those of them who weren't in a rocking chair in some nursing home in Des Moines or somewhere were probably doing the great jitterbug in the sky. "Maybe they're in their gardens too," I said.

She smiled and sighed. "Yes, probably."

Leaving Mrs Pritchard clipping her roses and chatting away to her dog, I walked back into the house, up the stairs and into my bedroom. I lay on my bed and thought of Mrs Pritchard and the American soldiers at some dance with a big band, having that good ole innocent black-and-white fun they used to have. I could hear the band, see the movement, the crew cuts, the laughing faces. It was only trying to imagine Mrs Pritchard as a girl that was causing the problems as I drifted off to sleep.

You know that superstrange feeling you get when you wake up in the afternoon after a heavy sleep? Now, imagine being in a room you don't recognize, bathed in sunlight, the only sound being the drowsy buzz of bees on the creepers outside my window.

It must have taken ten seconds for me to realize this wasn't another dream.

I got up, put on my sneakers and ambled along to the bathroom where I splashed some cold water on my face. Looking out of the window, I saw Mrs Pritchard, striding down the garden, carrying a bucket. She turned by the yew hedge and, from the direction of the pond, I heard her calling her ducks for their evening meal. I went downstairs.

It was hotter than ever when I walked out into the courtyard – a dry, still heat which seemed to hang in the air, stifling all the sound of the countryside. Even the birds seemed to be asleep.

I crossed the yard. There were no signs of the Hotshots and somehow I didn't have the energy for another conversation with Mrs Pritchard.

Outside the yard, a pathway led away from the buildings, through a small wood, up a hill.

I'm not usually one of the greatest walkers in the world but now, almost without thinking, I found myself wandering up the path.

After about a couple of hundred metres, I came to a small wooden gate, beyond which was a field. I opened it, went through – and found myself in the middle of a Tara nightmare. Everywhere I looked there were black and white cows, chewing, nodding their heads moodily to get rid of the flies. They stared at me without too much curiosity.

Keeping a careful eye on the cows, I made my way along the hedge beside the wood. There were rabbits by the side of the field which hopped away as I approached. From somewhere near by, a pigeon was cooing in a tree. Below me, I could see the drive and the Walkers' cottage. At the edge of the field was a small shed. I hesitated, curious as to what it was for, but then, seeing that there was a heavy padlock on the door, I continued on my walk.

As if I was in a dream, I moved along the edge of a field of golden waving corn that had yet to be harvested. It must have been twenty minutes since I left the house, when I reached a high hedge through which I could see a little country road. I seemed to have reached the edge of Mrs Pritchard's land.

I made my way along the hedge, looking for another way back to the house – a way which preferably wouldn't involve my getting lost or trampled to death by black and white cows. It was as I reached the corner of the wheatfield that I heard, beyond the hedge, a low murmur. It was a human voice.

I crouched down and edged my way forward. Through the branches I could see that there was a small pond beside the road.

A man with long, silvery hair sat with his back to where I was hidden. He seemed to be cross-legged, leaning forward, almost like someone at prayer. Then I saw that he was reading in a quiet melodic voice from a book.

There was a sigh from his left – a long, contented, female sigh. I shifted only slightly, but it was enough for me to see, a few feet away from the man, a pink blouse.

Hardly daring to breathe, I backed away.

I knew that blouse.

But what was it doing here?

CHAPTER EIGHT

Bedtime Story

You know the way that adults talk when they don't want children to hear what they're saying? It's a sort of lipless murmur, a frequency which you have to be a certain age to be able to pick up in your brain.

Well, my parents are into it.

Sometimes I'll be watching TV, or reading a magazine, when this mumbling sound comes from their direction.

"Hullo, I'm your daughter," I'll say sometimes. "I'm not like an enemy spy, you know."

"It's confidential," Daddy will say in his most annoying this-is-not-for-kids voice.

"It's not that you can't keep secrets," my mom will say. "It's that we don't want to burden you with them."

So maybe it's because I've got super-secretive parents that makes me really bad at keeping secrets myself. It's not that I'm a Chatty Cathy – I just like to share any information that happens to be going round.

"You'll never guess what I've just seen." I found Charlie, Lisa, Roberta and Tara in the sitting room when I returned.

"A rabbit?" said Roberta. "This place is like bunny farm."

"Maybe we should ask the old girl if we can borrow one of her guns," said Tara. "We could blast 'em."

"I can't believe that Ellie's made such friends with her," said Lisa, playing with her hair as usual. "They have these really long discussions about whether you should be allowed to chase foxes with dogs."

"It wasn't a rabbit," I said, trying to keep this conversation under control.

"Hounds." Charlie imitated the fruity accent of Mrs Pritchard. "We *never* call them dogs."

"I said I wasn't talking about rabbits."

"I reckon by the end of her stay here, Ellie won't be a veggie any more," said Roberta.

"And my allergies seem to be improving, too," said Charlie.

"Ding-dong!" I shouted. "*No rabbits!*"

"Rabbits? What's she talking about?" said Roberta to Lisa, as if I wasn't there.

"I saw Miss Billingham. She was beside a pond." I paused dramatically. "With a guy."

Now I had their attention.

"A guy? Miss B?" said Lisa.

"They were sitting together. It was kind of romantic, to tell the truth."

"Were they snogging?" asked Tara.

"Not exactly."

"Holding hands and staring into each other's eyes?" Lisa laughed. "That is so sweet."

"They weren't really doing that either."

"So what were they doing?" asked Charlie.

"He was reading a book to her."

"Oh, very romantic," said Lisa, losing interest.

"That explains everything," said Charlie. "Why she volunteered to come with us, why she's suddenly wearing make-up. Miss B's dating."

"What was he like?" asked Tara. "All sad and old and crusty and totally beyond?"

"I couldn't really see him," I said, reluctant to admit that Tara's description, except for the sad bit, was kind of accurate. "But I thought he looked really nice."

"Miss B in love," Roberta said quietly. "I've heard it all now."

Maybe it was the news about Miss Billingham, maybe the calm, warm weather – whatever the reason, a strange atmosphere seemed to descend on Cholmondley Manor that night.

We were laying the table in the kitchen when we saw Miss Billingham, walking quickly across the courtyard, her head down. One glance told me that she was rather less happy than when I had last seen her. She must have gone to her room because, five minutes later, she appeared in the kitchen.

To my amazement, she had changed back into the dull grey coat and shirt she used to wear in the library at Broadhurst. She seemed as pale as ever, the only sign of colour being a small rim of red around her eyes.

"Evening," she said in a voice that was not quite hers. "Sorry I'm late."

"You're not late, dear." Mrs Pritchard paused as she made some salad dressing. "These kind girls have been making me a vegetarian meal. They're trying to prove to me that I don't need to eat meat – rather late in the day, I fear."

"I went for a walk." Miss Billingham spoke as if she hadn't heard a word of what had been said. "Churches – I visited some churches." She sat down at the table and looked out of the window. "I love country churches, don't you?"

"Yeah," said Tara, leaning forward and carefully taking a tiny yellow flower that was caught in Miss Billingham's hair. "And churches are beyond flowery round here, aren't they?"

I dug Tara in the ribs. Miss Billingham took the flower, examined it for a moment as if one of life's great secrets was to be found in its petals. Suddenly, and without warning, her pale blue eyes were awash with tears.

Bottom line, it was the weirdest crying jag I've ever seen. She didn't sob or snuffle or look embarrassed – she just sat there, staring at that flower, tears coursing down her face.

"Well done, Tara," muttered Eve.

"Sorry, Miss B." Tara put a big hand on Miss Billingham's arm, but, as if we weren't there, the librarian continued to cry.

"Large drink, I think." Mrs Pritchard hadn't looked up from her work but somehow seemed to sense what was going on, wiped her hands and walked to a cupboard. "Brandy and ginger ale."

"She doesn't drink, actually," said Eve.

We all stared at Eve.

She shrugged defensively. "Well, she doesn't. Alcohol doesn't solve anything."

"Medical emergency." Mrs Pritchard put the drink she had made in front of Miss Billingham who was still slumped tragically, staring ahead of her. Zombie-like, she picked up the glass, took two deep swallows, put it down and gave a heartfelt sigh.

"Yeah, like she really doesn't drink," said Lisa.

Mrs Pritchard was putting the salad on the table. "Are we going to eat or not?" she said loudly.

"I'll drain the pasta," said Ellie.

"It's fettucine, Miss B." Eve spoke slowly, as if a few tears had robbed Miss Billingham of her knowledge of English. "You like that, don't you?"

"There's no need to patronize," murmured Roberta.

"Right." Mrs Pritchard took the large bowl of pasta from Ellie and put it on the table. "Here's Ellie's perfect meat-free meal. And here" – she walked to the fridge and took out a large bottle of white wine – "is something to wash it down. I think we're all in need of a little cheering up."

"We've got a match the day after tomorrow," said Eve, looking panicky.

"Get a life, Eve," muttered Lisa.

Smiling, Mrs Pritchard poured the wine, then raised her glass. "To the Hotshots," she said.

Uncertainly, we raised our glasses. "The Hotshots," we muttered."

"Bottoms up," said Lisa, just like her mum for a second.

"And to Mrs Pritchard," Ellie added. "We're really glad you invited us."

"I didn't actually invite you." Mrs Pritchard laughed. "To tell the truth, they had to bully me into taking you."

There was a moment's silence. Then Roberta came out

with the question that was in all of our minds. "They?" she asked. "Who's they?"

"My daughter. The Walkers. I thought it would be too much for me but they insisted. There was nowhere else for you to stay, apparently."

"Nowhere else? But . . ." and I was trying to get my head round this information. "We were told that you were happy to have us to stay."

"I am now. But then . . . I wasn't so sure. Particularly when Mary cancelled her visit at the last minute. She was going to help me out." She laughed again. "But you've been the perfect guests. Now tell me about this football thing that you play. I hope you don't kiss each other when you score a goal."

"No way," said Tara. "Kissing's for boys."

And so it went on. Football, boys, the countryside, the tournament – the combination of a glass of wine (in Tara's case, three glasses) and Mrs Pritchard's totally weird view of the world made the dinner speed by. By the end of the meal, even Miss Billingham was joining in now and then, in a deadpan, distant voice.

It was after we had finished Ellie's vegetarian extravaganza and had all helped with the washing-up that the conversation turned back to her once more.

We were in the sitting room, talking about the tournament (Mrs Pritchard: "Of course you'll win – everyone's hopeless at everything around here."), when Tara turned to Miss Billingham and, with her usual graceful tact, asked her how she thought we would do.

I guess we all noticed at the same time that, as Miss B reclined on the sofa, there were signs that the brandy and the wine she had drunk were getting to her. As she turned to look at us, she seemed to be shaking her head, the upper part of her body swaying slightly.

"Who'd like a bedtime story?" she asked in a quiet voice.

"Maybe tomorrow, dear," said Mrs Pritchard. "We've all had a very long day."

"I'm kind of tired," I said, and it was true – my head felt fuzzy, my limbs strange and heavy. Looking at the other Hotshots, I'd have bet money that they were feeling the same too.

"Yeah, I'd like a bedtime story," said Tara suddenly. "I'm really into stories."

"Well done, Tara," Eve murmured.

Leaning slightly forward where she sat, Miss Billingham started speaking.

"Once upon a time, there was a young girl. She lived in a big city. When she was at school in the sixth form, she met someone who changed her life. He was very tall and very handsome and very clever and he seemed to have read all the books in the world. They fell deeply in love."

"Ah, that's nice, Miss B," said Ellie. "Thanks for the—"

"But." Miss Billingham held up a hand as if she was about to make a solemn oath. "Everybody told the young girl that she was making a terrible mistake. They said, this man might be handsome and clever and all the things you say he is but he's too old for you. He's in his thirties and you're only eighteen. Then they said to the man, it's wrong for you to fall in love with a teenager. It will destroy your career. Did I tell you the man was the girl's teacher?"

We shook our heads.

"He was the girl's teacher. They parted. He left the city

and two years later he married someone else. She stayed in the town, and tried to live her life. But every day she thought of him at the beginning of her day. Every time she opened a book, she thought of him."

"I guess that's why she became a librarian," I said.

"Yes. She became a librarian." Miss Billingham sighed deeply. "One day, many years later, they met again. The man was as handsome and clever as he had ever been but he had grown a beard."

"Men with beards." Mrs Pritchard gave a shudder. "Yuk."

"They met and they talked and they found that, although they hadn't seen each other for twenty years, they were still deeply, deeply in love."

"But he was married," said Charlie.

"He had just got divorced but he loved his two teenage children very much and he was now a headmaster and he said that the last thing he needed in his life right now was a relationship and so it really was better that we didn't see each other because these things never work out second time around. We have separate lives, he said. We both have our careers. It wouldn't work out." Miss Billingham stood up. "So they both lived unhappily ever after," she whispered as she made her way slowly to the door.

"Goodnight, dear," said Mrs Pritchard.

"Yeah, and thanks for cheering us up," muttered Tara. "That's the most depressing bedtime story I've ever heard."

We looked at her in amazement.

"Coincidence it being about a librarian, wasn't it?" Tara continued.

"Hullo, ding-dong, she was talking about herself," said Roberta.

"Eh? Oh." Tara nodded slowly. "Oh, right."

"It's so sad," said Ellie. "We've got to help her."

"I think people have to work these things out for themselves," said Mrs Pritchard, getting to her feet with some difficulty. "Come on, Bournville – outies, then bed."

Upstairs, as we lay in our beds, I tried to talk to Tara about the evening's events. We had been so caught up in Miss Billingham's little drama that Mrs Pritchard's revelation over dinner had somehow been forgotten. We were at Cholmondley at the insistence of Mrs Fairbrother and the Walkers. Yet, now we were here, they had left us alone with the old lady. Their story was that they wanted to help the Hotshots. Mr and Mrs Psycho as caring, sharing football-lovers? It didn't make sense.

"I keep getting the feeling that we're being set up for something," I said.

Tara's reply took the form of snores.

I closed my eyes. Maybe it was the wine, or the emotion of Miss Billingham's bedtime story – whatever the reason, I slept well, and so did the others.

At some time during that night, it seemed to me that I heard a distant noise from the dark depths of the house – a thud, a strained, urgent whisper – but I was too tired to pay it any attention. I turned over and drifted off back to sleep.

CHAPTER NINE

Grown-up Time

"Something's happened."

It was Lisa who woke Tara and me. She was already dressed and looked paler than usual.

"Sheesh, my head," Tara groaned. "I'm never going to drink wine again."

"Me neither," said Lisa. "I had the weirdest dreams."

I sat up in bed and looked out of the window. The brightness of the sun briefly made my eyes ache.

"What's going on?" I asked Lisa.

"I heard men's voices. Mrs Pritchard sounds really angry about something."

We dressed quickly and went downstairs.

In the sitting room, Jim and Jill Walker were standing beside a young, uniformed policeman. Mrs Pritchard was on her knees in front of a chest of drawers.

"I know they were here," she was saying almost to herself. "I saw them."

"Is something wrong, Mrs Pritchard?" asked Ellie.

The old woman sat back. Apparently still wearing her nightdress under a dirty green gardening coat, she seemed frailer than usual this morning.

"Oh, someone's taken my silver, darling," she said. "All my photographs of my dogs and husband and horses. I kept them here." She waved a hand at the empty drawers. "Everything seems to have disappeared."

"Now, Mrs P, are you sure you put them there?" As usual, Mrs Walker spoke to her employer as if she was a little girl. "You know how forgetful you are."

"How could I forget moving about twenty silver frames?"

"Maybe they weren't there in the first place," said Jim Walker. "Remember that painting you said had been stolen? We found it in the attic, didn't we?"

"Ridiculous." Mrs Pritchard looked confused and lost. "Why on earth would I put a rather good Lionel Edwards in the attic?"

"We all do things which we forget we've done." Mrs Walker darted a bright, insincere smile in our direction. "Ain't that right, girls?"

Each of us was thinking, Er, no, but we mumbled agreement.

"When did you last see the silver, Mrs Pritchard?" asked the policeman in a voice so sympathetic that it was clear that he agreed with the Walkers' version of events.

"I don't know." Mrs Pritchard was looking under the chest of drawers, groping with her hand. "I don't know anything any more."

Mrs Walker sighed heavily. With a significant glance at the policeman, she tapped the side of her head.

The policeman closed the notebook in his hand and put it in his top pocket. "I suggest you have a good look for these things, madam. Maybe these young ladies could help you. Eh, girls?"

"Yes, of course," said Eve. "We'll organize a search."

"Who's he calling 'ladies'?" said Tara in a loud whisper.

Jill Walker was standing over Mrs Pritchard. "Let's go and have a nice cup of tea," she said, helping Mrs Pritchard to her feet. The old woman looked around her as if at last accepting that her imagination had been playing tricks on her after all. Resting on Mrs Walker's arm, she made her way slowly towards the door.

"I don't mind the guns. It's the photographs I care about," she muttered.

"Guns?" said Roberta.

"She thinks she's lost a pair of shotguns," said Mrs Walker as if Mrs Pritchard couldn't hear what she was saying. "Poor old dear. They were sold last year."

Mrs Pritchard shook her head. "I was sure they were there."

"Not for months, Mrs P." Mr Walker gave a tolerant little laugh.

"They weren't sold." The old lady shook her head irritably. "They were my late husband's. Why on earth would I have sold them?"

"I'll be on my way," said the policeman.

"Thanks so much," said Mrs Walker. "Sorry we bothered you for nothing."

"Cheers, mate," said Mr Walker.

"Excuse me." Ellie spoke with quiet firmness. "But where were the guns kept?"

"Listen, love, this is grown-up time." Mr Walker was

smiling but his eyes betrayed a certain irritation. "This officer's rather too busy to play kid detective."

"I am not your 'love'," Ellie said coldly. Turning to Mrs Pritchard, she asked, "Where did you keep the guns?"

"Downstairs Gents."

"Behind the door."

"Yes. That's where they've been for years."

Ellie looked up at the policeman. "I saw them there yesterday evening."

"Was that after your glass of wine?" asked Mr Walker.

But the policeman had produced his little book and, in slow, careful handwriting he was making a note. "How many guns were there?" he asked.

"Two," said Ellie without a moment's hesitation.

"What kind were they?"

"I don't know . . ."

Jim seemed about to interrupt but Ellie fixed him with her coolest stare.

" . . . and I don't care, because I'm not exactly interested in murdering animals. They each had these two long, shiny barrels. I remember thinking how weird it was that all that care and beauty had gone into making machines that were for killing things."

"She's right." Tara spoke up. "I saw them too."

"My husband's two Purdeys," said Mrs Pritchard. "They were twelve-bore shotguns. She's described them perfectly."

The policeman was tapping his notebook. "Perhaps I could have a word with you girls," he said.

*

Bottom line, there didn't seem to be much to tell PC Smethurst, as he was called. Ellie's snooping hadn't got much further than the downstairs loo and Tara's powers of observation weren't exactly impressive. We mentioned that Mrs Pritchard had seemed worried that things were disappearing, but PC Smethurst showed little interest. As far as he was concerned, the only thing the old lady had lost was her marbles.

The guns interested him slightly more. We followed as Ellie took him to the downstairs toilet. Behind the door was a glass-fronted cabinet which PC Smethurst inspected for a moment. "No fingerprints," he murmured to himself. "And no sign that the lock has been forced." He made a note. "We've had a few thefts of guns recently. We'll make a few inquiries." He glanced at his watch. "There's no one you've seen around the place, acting suspiciously, is there?"

Nervously, I put up a hand. "The night before last I couldn't sleep and I came downstairs and I thought I saw someone moving about."

PC Smethurst looked at me, his notebook firmly shut.

"I thought it was a ghost but . . . maybe it wasn't," I ended lamely.

"It was Mrs Pritchard," said Charlie. "She told us she goes for midnight walks."

I was thinking that the midnight rambler moved too fast for any old lady, even Mrs Pritchard, but a look of weary indifference had returned to PC Smethurst's face.

"And you haven't talked to anyone in the town about this place?" he asked casually.

We shook our heads, looking at one another.

"Don't stare at me," said Tara suddenly and, for the first

time, I noticed that her cheeks were bright red – a sure sign that she's feeling guilty. "I ain't done nothing."

There was silence for a moment.

Tara's one of those people who, if they're in trouble, will somehow manage to make things worse. Now she swore angrily. "Since when has it been against the law to talk to people?"

"What are you on about, Tara?" asked Eve.

"You know what I'm on about," snapped Tara. "Just because I talked to that gang in the town, you think . . ." She looked away angrily. "So what if I told them I was staying here? You lot are so sad – it always has to be my fault whenever anything goes wrong." With a few muttered swear words, she fell silent.

I closed my eyes. Bigstuff. Chummy Manor. It wouldn't have taken much for him to have found out where we were staying.

PC Smethurst had opened his notebook again. He turned back to Tara. "Now, miss. Perhaps you'd care to tell me more about your friends in the town," he said with a polite, pale smile.

CHAPTER TEN

Creepers

So Tara had talked to a few guys on motorbikes in the town. Was that enough to make us the bad guys of Cholmondley Manor? Apparently it was.

After the policeman left, we ate breakfast in the kitchen. Mrs Pritchard seemed to have been taken back to her bedroom but now and then Jill Walker strutted about the room, filling kettles and rinsing dishes in a busy, self-important way. For most of the time she ignored us but now and then darted an irritated look in our direction, as if to remind us that, until the Hotshots had hit town, everything had been just fine.

We had been in the kitchen only a few minutes before Miss Billingham wafted in, looking as pale and tragic as a ghost. The news, during the night, that there had been a break-in, probably caused by one of the girls she was meant to be looking after, caused only the tiniest tremor of interest on her face.

"I don't understand," she said in a distant voice.

"The police gave me an extreme hard time," said Tara, who was beginning to enjoy the drama of the occasion. "I reckon I could be done as an accessory."

"Police?" Miss Billingham's face turned even paler. "The police are involved?"

For a moment, we looked at one another despairingly, each of us thinking that, if this was what true love did to the brain, we'd be steering clear of it. "Ding-dong," said Roberta quietly.

It was as we tried, using very short sentences and simple words, to explain the seriousness of the situation to the lovestruck librarian, that Jim Walker walked in carrying a tray. "The boss is on her way," he said, bundling plates and cups into the sink as if he actually wanted to break them. "You girls better make yourselves scarce."

"Mrs Pritchard doesn't mind us being here," said Ellie.

"The real boss." Hands on hips, Walker stood over us at the table. "The person who arranged your little visit. Mrs Fairbrother." Seeing that we looked confused, he added, "The old girl's her mother, ain't she? She's concerned."

"Poor Mrs Pritchard," said Eve. "She looked so upset."

"Gone, more like." Walker gave an unpleasant little laugh. "She's been imagining things for months, poor old bat. This has been coming for a long time."

Ellie was frowning. "But she didn't imagine this," she said. "Those guns were here yesterday – I saw them. And if the guns were stolen, why shouldn't other things have—?"

"It's complicated, right?" Walker interrupted. "Take 'em off to play football, will you, love?" he said to Miss Billingham. "They've done enough damage already."

"We have?" said Charlie angrily.

Miss Billingham was stirring her tea slowly. "Dear oh dear," she said hopelessly.

There was something threatening in the way Jim Walker was looking at us.

"Let's go for a walk," I said quickly. "We could go up the hill and I could show you the pond where I saw . . . Er, where I saw the ducks."

"I think you should go into town," said Walker. "Do a bit of practice. Hang around. Do anything you like so long as you keep out of the way."

Jill Walker walked in. "She's still going on about guns," she murmured to her husband. "Getting in a proper state."

"I tell you, she's gone." He glanced in our direction. "Poor old girl."

We washed up our plates, then went to fetch our kit from our rooms. As the others joined Miss Billingham at the front door, a thought occurred to me. I walked quickly to the downstairs bathroom. Carefully I opened the glass-fronted door of the gun cabinet and looked inside. There was a faint smell of oil. I ran my finger along the green felt at the base of the cupboard. Unmistakably, there were two smallish indentations in the felt where the guns would have rested.

The smell of oil. Marks in the felt. I'm not exactly Sherlock Holmes but I'd have laid money that the guns had been there – and recently.

Frankly, the buzz had gone. Mrs Pritchard was in her room going bananas. Miss Billingham was in some la-la land of magical romance. Tara was steaming because the cops seemed to be blaming everything on her. Mr and Mrs Psycho Walker had rolled up the welcome mat some time ago. The mysterious Mrs Fairbrother was on her way.

"I wanna go home," mumbled Roberta as we trudged down the lane to catch the bus.

"Yeah, who needs football?" said Lisa. "Let's just grab a train and pretend none of this happened."

"The countryside." Tara looked at the fields around her as if she was standing in the middle of a municipal rubbish tip. "I told you the countryside was lame."

We walked in silence for a few seconds.

"What d'you think, Stevie?" Lisa had that bright, dangerous look on her face – the look that means she's out for blood. "After all, it was your brilliant idea that got us here in the first place."

I tried a smile. "There's only one more day," I said. "We should just play our football and go home. Anyway, until this morning, I was having a good time. We all were."

Lisa glanced back at Miss Billingham, trailing along behind us like a ghost. "Having a good time? I don't think so," she said.

"Yeah, and if I see one more field, I'm going to be sick," said Tara.

"Hey, guys, let's just be positive, shall we?" I pleaded.

"Paaarsitive," went Tara. "Bloomin' Yank."

We had reached the bus stop and stood, by the side of the small country road, waiting in silence for the little green bus to arrive. At least, I thought to myself, it can't get worse than this.

Er, wrong.

When we arrived in Oakmere, the town was full of

people. In the square, stalls had been set up and people were selling everything from vegetables to old bits of furniture.

"Market day!" Miss Billingham clasped her hands in front of her. "How romantic!"

"This is where they come to sell their wives," said Tara loudly.

Charlie and Roberta started laughing.

"It is."

Miss Billingham was smiling. "I never knew you were a Hardy fan, Tara," she said.

"Who does he play for?"

"There's this wonderful novel called *The Mayor of Casterbridge*. In it, Michael Henchard gets drunk and takes his poor wife and child to market. I love reading Thomas Hardy."

"Shut up Thomas Hardy," muttered Tara. "It wasn't a book. It was a film – a lame one, too."

"Sorry to interrupt this intellectual discussion," said Lisa. "But maybe we should go to the training ground."

Miss Billingham had begun to look tragic again. "I was hoping to look round the market," she said.

"We could all do that, then train later," said Roberta.

I glanced at Miss Billingham. "I think maybe Miss B wants to shop alone," I said.

"Yes," she said. "I suddenly feel like being . . . alone. That would be nice."

For a few seconds, we stood there – just so that she knew we weren't fooled for one second by her little act.

She sighed. "What shall we say? An hour? Back here? Fine."

She wandered off and was soon lost in the crowd.

"Charming," said Roberta. "She's off for another snog with her boyfriend."

"Actually, librarians don't snog," said Eve in her most serious voice. "They read to one another."

Laughing, we made our way across the market place towards the sports ground.

Although an adult football team was training at one end of the ground, we could see there was enough room to play a game of one-touch in a corner of the pitch. I was relieved to see that Bigstuff and his pals were nowhere to be seen.

"Hi." Lisa entered the clubhouse ahead of the rest of us and shared her Hollywood smile with Mr Gibson, the ground manager, who was drying some glasses behind the small bar.

He looked rather less than totally overjoyed to see us.

"Ah, yes, girls." He put down the glass he had been shining and smiled nervously. "What a surprise."

"We thought we'd have a little extra practice," said Charlie. "If that's all right with you."

Gibson was looking nervously out of the window. "There may be a small problem," he said in a low voice. "In fact, without putting too fine a point on it, your presence here poses certain logistical problems of a security nature."

"What's he banging on about?" Tara asked of no one in particular.

"Security?" said Eve. "Are you saying that you don't trust us?"

"No no." Gibson licked his thin lips and darted another glance in the direction of the pitch. "It's not you. It's . . . your supporters."

Supporters? We looked at one another.

"It's Tara's friends." Ellie spoke from the window. "There's a whole load of bikers in the car park beyond the pitch."

We moved towards her but Gibson was quick to usher us away from the window. "Don't let them see you," he hissed.

"Hang on, we're not criminals," said Charlie. "What's going on?"

"The police have been asking questions," said Gibson. "Something about a break-in. For some reason, the kids think you had something to do with their being blamed."

"Oh terrific," said Lisa. "Now it's all our fault."

"Shut up our fault." Tara was standing near the door, her face dark with anger. "My fault, you mean. I'm going to sort those guys." Before any of us could stop her, she had turned, left the clubhouse and was walking briskly towards the bikers.

"Oh dear," Gibson muttered. "This is just the kind of scenario I wanted to avoid. She won't make things worse, your friend, will she?"

Lisa gave an exaggerated wince. "Tara make things worse? Never!"

By now, Tara had reached the group and was standing in front of them. As they saw who it was, they had stopped talking and seemed alert, ready for anything. She stood in front of them, her brightly coloured tracksuit looking small against the dark semicircle of menace.

"I'm going to help her," said Eve.

"No!" There was panic in Gibson's voice. "That'll make it worse. If your friend just explains the situation calmly and coolly, we might just avoid an unpleasant incident."

Calmly? Coolly? Tara? The guy had just made up our minds for us. Ignoring his pleas, we left the clubhouse and made our way towards the action.

"Gunfight at Oakmere Football Club," joked Roberta, but none of us laughed.

Ghosts, robbers, broken hearts and now a gangland rumble. A fine trip to the countryside this was turning out to be.

As we approached, the sound of Tara's version of diplomacy – consisting mainly of words my father calls "inappropriate expletives" – reached us. Bigstuff stood in front of the bikers, chewing gum, unsmiling. Somehow I didn't think Tara had won him over with her natural girlish charm.

"These guys are chiefing me out," she shouted as we joined her. "They're saying we grassed them up to the rozzers. No way would I grass anyone up. Not my worst enemy. Never. On my mother's life."

Bigstuff stepped forward and stood a yard in front of Tara, hands in the pockets of his leather jacket. "Someone told the police we had done over some house. They've been giving us grief all day. My mum asked them who'd knocked us. They said, 'The London girls'."

Before anyone could stop her, Eve stepped forward – small, neat, irritating. "Actually," she said in a voice like the squeaky-clean heroine of an old-fashioned movie, "all that we told the police was that you knew where we were staying. If you're so innocent, I'm sure you'll have absolutely nothing to worry about."

Bad move. The temperature seemed to crank up a few more degrees.

"Listen up, girls," Bigstuff said with a sneer in his voice. "Maybe down in London, the police believe you when you say you're innocent but, round here, they need just this excuse to bring you in." He lifted his right hand, stained with oil, as if holding something almost invisibly tiny between his big thumb and forefinger, then slowly clenched the hand into a fist.

"Don't threaten us." It was the strong, confident voice of Charlie. "Unless you want real problems with the police."

Like magic, a police car pulled up on the road yards away from where we stood. Two uniformed officers got out, pulling on their peaked caps in that we're-the-big-guys-round-here way of theirs.

"Here come your friends," said one of Bigstuff's girls.

"Yeah, they've got their own little police escort," said another biker.

The policemen were distinctly less friendly than PC Smethurst had been. "Is there some kind of problem here?" the older of the two asked.

"Just talking about tomorrow's game." Bigstuff winked unpleasantly at Tara. "Eh, girlie?"

There was a moment's silence. Then, before Tara or Eve could say anything to make the situation worse than it was, I spoke up. "We were just about to do a training session for tomorrow's game," I said with an attempt at a smile. "Is that OK, officer?"

"I don't think so," said the policeman. "If I were you, I'd keep away from the ground."

"Until tomorrow," I said.

"I'd keep away from the ground," the policeman repeated in a bored voice. "We weren't in favour of inviting incomers to the tournament anyway. After all the problems last year." He glanced at Bigstuff and his friends, then turned back to us. "If you want my advice, you'll go home."

Reluctantly, we began to move away, watched by the policemen and the bikers.

"Running away, girls?" Bigstuff called out in a mocking voice. "Just when we were going to have some spiffing fun with you."

Yeah. Like we really believed that.

Bottom line, we were shaken by what had happened. Even Tara, who's kind of used to dealing with thugs and policemen, was quiet as we made our way back into town. However heavy things had become back at the old manor, I guess we had all been thinking that the tournament would be an easygoing, light-hearted occasion where we could forget our troubles. Suddenly, the game tomorrow had begun to seem like our biggest problem.

"This is so what I don't need," Lisa muttered.

"I?" said Ellie. "I thought we were meant to be in this together."

"Yeah, but some of us haven't been hanging out with local knuckleheads."

"Not my fault," snapped Tara. "How was I to know they were creepers?"

"Creeps, not creepers," said Eve irritably. "Try to get that right at least."

"Shut up creeps," said Tara. "Creepers are like burglars who do houses when people are there. You've got creepers and twocers and—"

"Twocers?" said Charlie.

"Yeah, TWOC – taking without owner's consent. Car thieves, to you. Sheesh, don't you guys know anything?"

"Sorry, Tara. We're not quite as well educated as you," said Lisa with a sarcastic smile.

"OK, cool it, right," I interrupted. There was something about the Hotshots these days that made me so mad. In the early days, we used to stick together when the world outside turned mean. Now we did nothing but bicker. I must have shouted because, as I stood there in the High Street, they were all looking at me. "Let's just . . . figure out what we're going to do now. We can worry about the game later."

"Do? We hang around this dump until Miss Billingham turns up," said Lisa.

"With Oakmere's lost boys looking out for us? I don't think so," I said. "The cop told us to get out of town."

"Charming," said Roberta.

"I suggest that some of us go home, the rest wait for Miss B," I said.

"So that way only some of us really get beaten up. Great idea, Stevie," said Ellie.

"Think about it," I said. "It's Tara they're really after . . ." I paused as Tara pranced around shadow-boxing for a couple of seconds. "If a couple of us went back to the

89

house and the rest of you hung around the market place, there shouldn't be any trouble."

This logical plan caused the usual five-minute debate before Charlie spoke up in its favour. Suddenly (why is it that Charlie has this effect and I don't?) it was the most terrific idea that had ever been thought of. Ellie, Tara and I would take the bus home. The others would kill time drinking Cokes at a nearby hamburger bar.

There was one other thing that had been bothering me all day. Why had the Walkers been so anxious to convince the policeman that Mrs Pritchard had dreamt up the break-in?

"Maybe you could call Jamie," I said casually to Eve.

"Why not?" She smiled. "He'll enjoy news of our latest disaster."

"That uncle of his – the journalist who works on the *Star*. Perhaps he could see if there's anything on the computer about the Walkers."

Eve frowned. "The Walkers? You know something about them?"

I shook my head. "There's just something not quite right about them."

"Oh great," joked Roberta. "Now Stevie wants to get the Walkers on our case, too."

"Will you ask him?" I said to Eve.

She shrugged. "OK, Sherlock," she said.

CHAPTER ELEVEN

Megaflop

Looking back, I can see that the way Ellie, Tara and I returned to Cholmondley Manor might look kind of sneaky but I swear that what we did, what we discovered, was an accident.

The sun was beating down. None of us were feeling exactly full of conversation. In that dry, dead heat, there was a sort of heaviness in the air. The birds weren't singing and the only sound to be heard was that of our feet as we padded down the hard, dusty drive towards the house.

We noticed a big car, some kind of Daimler or Jaguar, outside the front door and, for the first time, it occurred to us that returning ahead of schedule hadn't been the greatest of ideas. Not wanting to disturb Mrs Pritchard, we cut across the front lawn and through the small white gate which led to the kitchen door via a small orchard.

It was only as we made our way through the apple trees that we realized what a bad move this was.

There were voices ahead of us, a man's and a woman's, speaking in those clipped, well-bred English tones that are never raised but which can somehow cut like glass. Now and then another voice, a low, weary murmur, could be heard.

We froze, looking at one another helplessly. If we turned back and were seen slinking away through the gate, it would seem as if we had been spying. Yet blundering on, appearing out of the trees like magic seemed kind of impolite, too.

So we waited. In those fateful moments, we only heard a few words but they were enough.

Mother. Home. Time. Own good. Leave. Home. Too much. Unfair on us. Home. Please, mother. Home.

I decided to act. "Yeah, that was why I played the ball to you—" Speaking at the top of my voice, I moved through the trees. For a moment, Tara and Ellie looked at me in astonishment. Then I waved my arms like a conductor trying to stir an orchestra into life. "Then you passed to Lisa, right. And she—"

"Oh yes," said Ellie suddenly. "She dummied the defender. Oh!"

She gave a brilliantly convincing start of surprise. Ahead of us, sitting in the shade of a tree, sat three people – a man and a woman I had never seen before and, between them, Mrs Pritchard.

"Hello," I said innocently. "I'm sorry – we didn't realize you were here."

Tara was pushing her way through branches behind us. "What you talking about dummies?" she said loudly. "We didn't even play football in town." She smiled broadly at Mrs Pritchard. "Yo, Mrs P, how ya doin'?"

"Hello, girls." The old woman smiled wearily and I noticed that she seemed paler than normal, as if the events of the previous twelve hours had aged her.

Despite the heat, the woman sitting to Mrs Pritchard's right was wearing some kind of tweed skirt. For a moment, she stared at us with undisguised irritation. "You must be the Hotshots," she said. "We weren't expecting you back until this afternoon."

"There was kind of a snafu at the sports ground," I said.

"Snafu?"

"Yeah," said Tara. "Situation normal another—"

"Foul-up," I said quickly. "There was a sort of misunder-standing between us and some . . . friends."

"Well, it's very nice to see you, girls." Mrs Pritchard managed a smile. "This is my daughter, Mrs Fairbrother, and her husband."

"Hi."

"Hello."

"Yo."

Our three greetings didn't seem to impress the Fairbrothers.

"We were having a family discussion," said Mr Fair-brother, a tall, sandy-haired guy with those cold, impassive eyes which a certain kind of Englishman has. "A confiden-tial family discussion."

"We didn't hear anything," Tara blurted out. "And even if we had, we wouldn't tell anyone. But we didn't, so . . . it doesn't matter anyway."

There's something about Tara that has this effect on people – a sort of impression of guilt that hangs about her, even on those rare occasions when she is completely innocent. Mr and Mrs Fairbrother looked at us with undis-guised suspicion.

"There are some biscuits on the kitchen table." Mrs

93

Pritchard's voice was cracked and frail. "Why not go and tuck in?"

We thanked her and, with a few polite nods and smiles, moved off towards the house. As we left, I glanced over my shoulder. Mr and Mrs Fairbrother had turned to Mrs Pritchard and were talking in urgent, low voices. The old woman sat back in her seat, her head slumped forward, her eyes closed, a picture of misery.

"Nice family," I murmured.

Some of the most difficult moments of my life have been played to the background tune of knives and forks clinking on china. There was the dinner on the day when my mother had been promoted to the job at the bank my father had wanted. Or the breakfast when Mom suddenly announced that they were thinking of taking me away from Broadhurst Comprehensive to be with "nice girls" at a boarding school. There was the first time Lisa came for a meal and drank out of the fingerbowl. I tell you, I could write a full-length book called *Disastrous Meals I Have Known*.

And right up there with the dining megaflops of all time would be that evening's meal at Cholmondley Manor.

It wasn't that the food was bad. Compared to Mrs Pritchard's efforts, the chicken casserole produced by Mrs Fairbrother was the ultimate in haute cuisine. It was the company that was the problem.

When the other four Hotshots returned from the town with Miss Billingham, it was obvious that the course of true love hadn't exactly been running smooth that day. The librarian's eyes were red from crying and her general mood

94

of gloom had somehow infected each of them – even Lisa, whose ego is usually like a bullet-proof vest against other people's problems, was quiet and almost thoughtful.

Unhappy love affairs, something weird happening between Mrs Pritchard and her daughter, and, for us, the thought of a tournament the next day against a team that now totally hated us – I guess it was hardly surprising that, while the evening sun still shone outside, the temperature around the table was arctic.

"Not for me, thanks." Ellie may have been trying her polite smile as a steaming plate of chicken flesh was placed in front of her but she only managed a wince of distaste. "I'm a vegetarian."

"Don't be ridiculous," said Mrs Fairbrother spooning out the next helping. "You're in the country now. It's no place for fussy doers."

Ellie passed the plate to me. "I'm not fussy. I just don't believe in the slaughter of innocent animals to provide food for humans."

"I've never heard anything so absurd in all my born days." Mrs Fairbrother frowned as she scooped some vegetables from the casserole and splashed them onto a plate which she put down firmly in front of Ellie.

"I won't, thanks." Ellie spoke quietly. "The vegetables have been in contact with the meat juice."

Mrs Fairbrother muttered something under her breath.

"I'm very happy with cereal," said Ellie.

"Nobody has cereal for dinner. You can watch us eat, then do what you like later. Frankly you girls have caused quite enough problems already."

We looked at one another in astonishment. Now what

had we done wrong? Normally one of us would have spoken up but there was something about Mrs Fairbrother that discouraged conversation.

"Eat up, girls," she said with a cold smile. One by one we picked up our knives and forks and began to eat. Ellie stared at her plate, a hint of tears in the corners of her eyes. "You need building up."

There was a sort of angry mutter from the head of the table where Mrs Pritchard was sitting. She pushed back her chair, dabbed at her mouth with a napkin, then, without a word, left the room.

"Mother!" snapped Mrs Fairbrother. "Where are you going?"

Moments later, the old woman returned, carrying a bowl brimming with cereal and a jug of milk, which she put in front of Ellie, taking away her plate of polluted vegetables.

"Thank you," Ellie mumbled.

"Principles," said Mrs Pritchard, returning to her chair. "I may not agree with them but I like a girl who has principles."

Mrs Fairbrother laughed harshly. "Have you ever seen a cow when her calf is taken from her?" she asked Ellie. "She bellows for days – just so that you can enjoy that milk of yours. Now that's what I call cruel."

"Be quiet, Mary," said Mrs Pritchard with a flash of anger we had never seen in her before. "Stop being such a bully."

"Let's all eat up." Mr Fairbrother spoke up for the first time. "I, for one, am starving."

We had been eating in awkward silence for a few moments when Mrs Fairbrother spoke again. "Now that we've sorted out the dietary arrangements" – she shot a lethal glance in Ellie's direction – "I have something rather more important to discuss with you all. Earlier this evening I had a call from the Oakmere Constabulary. They'd rung my housekeeper in London to get the number of my mobile telephone, so I knew it was important. And it was." She paused dramatically. "They want you to withdraw from the tournament tomorrow."

There were confused protests from around the table.

"No way," Tara said loudly. "We ain't done nothing wrong."

"It appears that certain local elements do not agree that you 'ain't done nothing wrong'. There was a certain incident at the sports ground today, was there not?"

"There's this gang. They think we got them into trouble." I spoke quickly to forestall another explosion from Tara. "We discussed it with them. The police came along and said it wasn't a very good idea to practise."

"Yes. And, after you left, the police heard that the locals planned to disrupt the tournament tomorrow if you play."

"Charming," said Roberta faintly.

"But that's not our fault," I protested. "Tara's right. We haven't done anything wrong."

"Of course, you're right in a sense." Mr Fairbrother spoke in his best reasonable-guy voice. "But the fact is, the police know these people. They've been involved in gang violence on the coast. It appears" – he smiled wanly – "that their bite is every bit as bad as their bark."

"Big deal." Tara seemed almost to be enjoying this. "The Hotshots don't scare that easy."

"Are there any alternatives?" asked Miss Billingham.

Mrs Fairbrother shrugged. "It's advice, not an order," she said. "They say they can't guarantee your safety. The responsible thing would be to return to London tomorrow. Put your trip to the countryside down to experience."

"Wouldn't that be kind of admitting defeat?" I asked.

"You can't win 'em all," said Mr Fairbrother briskly. "There's a train for London that leaves just after ten tomorrow."

"No way," Tara repeated in a quiet, determined way. "We came to play football and that's what we're going to do." She looked around the table. "Right?"

None of us replied. Possibly for the first time in history, the Hotshots were lost for words.

It was late, but not too late. After everyone had gone to bed, I waited an hour or so, then crept downstairs. For a change, I was in luck. Mrs Fairbrother's mobile telephone was lying on the hall table. I picked it up, crept to the kitchen, closed the door and dialled.

"Could I speak to Jamie, please?"

As usual, the O'Keeffe family were making a late night of it. Jamie's mum expressed no surprise at my midnight call and shouted for him. Moments later, he was on the line.

"Stevie, what's happened?"

"Kind of nothing and everything. Did you check out the Walkers?"

"Yeah. My uncle let me come into his office to look them up on the London crime report database. There were a few Jim Walkers, but none of them fitted the description. Then I checked out a Paul Walker, done for aggravated burglary in this area ten years ago. He had previous convictions and was given a two-year sentence."

"Er, wrong name, Jamie."

"His full name was Paul James Walker. He fits your description, except at that time he had a beard."

"Different name. Beard. Kind of a long shot, isn't it?"

"Right, that's what I thought at first. I was about to give up when I noticed the name of the magistrate who tried the case." Jamie lowered his voice so that at first I couldn't catch the name. When he repeated it, I was as confused as ever.

Mr Charles Fairbrother.

CHAPTER TWELVE

Out of our Depth

I awoke early, my mind already full of what I had to do. I shook Tara awake. After a bit of swearing, she opened her eyes.

"What's going on?" She looked out of the window. A heavy summer mist had concealed even the farm buildings across the courtyard from the house. "What time is it?"

"Seven o'clock." Ignoring Tara's protests, I told her about my call to Jamie.

"Still don't see why I have to get up early," she grunted.

"You will." I stripped back her bedclothes. "You coming or not?"

"Bloomin' Yank." Tara sat up on the side of the bed and groped for her clothes.

Outside, the fog was so thick that the only way I could find my way was by following the drive, then the path up the hill. Once we were some way from the house, we talked quietly, our voices sounding muffled and strange. Although it was light, it was impossible to see more than a few yards in front of us.

"It's like white night," Tara said as we reached the field

at the top of the hill. There was an uncertainty in her voice, almost a hint of fear.

I led her along the hedge, but instead of turning left towards the pond where I had seen Miss Billingham, we kept straight on. Below us, some two hundred yards or so to our right, would be the small cottage where the Walkers lived. No way were we going near there. Our destination was a small shed on the verge of woods ahead of us.

"A shed?" Tara gave a disbelieving laugh when we found it. "You got me out of bed to look at a bloomin' toolshed? You are beyond weird, Stevie."

"It's not a toolshed. It's stuck in the corner of a field – it must have been for keeping feed for animals."

"Yeah, and that is so not what I need to hear at seven in the morning."

"I noticed it the other day." I walked to the side of the shed where there was a small window. Inside the smudged, dirty panes of glass, strong wire netting could be seen. "I've been thinking about it. Why should someone want to make a shed in the middle of nowhere so secure?" I moved to the door. A heavy chain hung between two cast iron loops, fastened by a big industrial padlock.

"It's new," said Tara. "No way are we getting into this shed without a key."

I looked at the roof, hoping to find a loose slat, but now I saw it was covered by sheet metal which had been screwed to the wood. I took a torch out of my pocket and moved to the window.

"Sheesh, quite the little girl guide, aren't you?" laughed Tara.

I shone the light into the gloom inside the shed. It was

difficult to see anything through the murk. "There are sacks on the ground," I whispered.

"Big wow," muttered Tara. "You mean the feed shed's got sacks of feed. Come on, let's get out of here."

"Look!" The torchlight had caught the glint of something in the corner. Pressing my face to the glass, I could make out a shape.

"Stevie." Tara was nudging me.

"It's the guns," I said. "I can see the silver stuff on the side of them. There's one and—"

"Er, Stevie."

It was then I heard a sound that made my heart skip a beat. A loud, confident male cough.

Slowly, I turned.

The figure stood motionless ten yards away from us, the fog swirling around giving it a strange ghostly look.

"Haven't you done enough harm?" The voice was Walker's. It sounded quiet and disappointed, yet heavy with threat. "You've nearly killed a nice old lady with your meddling. Now you're snooping around her property."

"Sorry," I muttered. "We weren't—"

"You just listen to me." Walker lowered his voice until it was almost a whisper. "Here's what you do. You go back to the house. You say nothing of what you've seen. You pack your bags. You catch that train. Understood?"

"Yeah, right," said Tara.

"You're out of your depth, girls. If you don't take my advice . . ." Walker sighed, as if reluctant to continue. "Something really quite serious might happen. That's the trouble with life in the country. Accidents do happen and there's no one around to see who caused them."

"We just wanted to play football," I said.

"This is not a game." The figure turned and walked slowly down the hill until the fog had swallowed him up. Through the greyness, the words drifted up to us once more. "Not a game." Then he was gone.

For a moment we stood there, breathing heavily.

"Cheers, Jimmy," Tara said eventually. "And the top of the morning to you, too."

She laughed briefly, but when I looked at her, I noticed she was trembling.

The words "Hotshots" and "planning" go together like "honest" and "politician", or "witty" and "teacher" or "heatwave" and "British". Fact is, we do things first, then start thinking about the consequences.

But now there was no avoiding it. We had to make a plan.

"We just got threatened by Psycho." Tara burst into the room occupied by Lisa, Roberta and Charlie. On our way back to the house, she had seemed to have recovered from our meeting in the fog and was now as fired up as ever. "It was beyond scary, man."

The girls sat up in their beds. Ignoring Tara, I fetched Ellie and Eve from next door and brought them up to date.

"I called Jamie last night on Mrs Fairbrother's mobile."

"Sheesh." Lisa gave a little laugh. "Taking a bit of a risk, weren't you?"

"I had to. Jamie's discovered that a Paul James Walker was sent to jail by Mr Fairbrother. I reckon it's Psycho and that he's the one who's been stealing stuff from Mrs Pritchard – maybe for revenge against the Fairbrothers."

"He'd recognize him," said Roberta.

"Ten years ago?" I said. "And, according to the press report, Walker had a beard then."

"Yeah, and, as from this morning, he knows that we've discovered what's in his little shed," said Tara.

"We're outta here." Lisa spoke decisively. "We're in way over our heads. Let's catch that train back home and try to forget all about it."

We were sitting in gloomy silence when there was a light knock at the door. It was Miss Billingham, and she had a large envelope in her hand. "Postman," she said. She handed the envelope to me. It was addressed to "The Hotshots, Cholmondley Manor, Oakmere, Suffolk".

Frowning, I tore it open. "It's a good-luck card," I said faintly. The others gathered round. The card had been signed by each of our parents. Even Moonie Morley had contributed a jokey "Broadhurst Comprehensive expects . . . Come on, you Hotshots!"

As the card was passed around, each of us looked at it with the good cheer of a prisoner reading his own death warrant.

"We can't do it," I said finally. "We can't go back home and tell them we ran away."

"Mrs Fairbrother said it was the responsible thing to do," said Lisa.

"Responsible to who?" said Charlie. "Whenever adults talk about responsibility, it means doing something that suits them."

"Remember that song we used to sing in the Met Cup?" Ellie spoke up. "All about 'We are Hotshots, No one likes us, We don't care'? I guess it's true now."

"The Fairbrothers, the police, Bigstuff – it's us against the world," said Roberta.

There was silence in the room for a moment.

"It sounds to me as if you've made up your minds," said Miss Billingham.

"What d'you think we should do, Miss B?" asked Eve.

"I think . . ." Miss Billingham winked. "I think – come on, you Hotshots!"

I stood up. "Let's go and make Mrs Fairbrother's day," I said.

As we made our way downstairs, I noticed that Miss Billingham was smiling to herself.

It was only later, when we were on the bus taking us to the Oakmere Tournament, that we discovered the real reason she was so pleased about our decision.

CHAPTER THIRTEEN

The Love-hooligan

"I can see Stephen once more."

So strange had our trip to the countryside become that our journey to Oakmere seemed to us no more than normally weird. We were on a little single-decker bus winding its way through country roads. The only other passengers were an old couple who sat on the back seat of the bus ignoring each other and us as they stared ahead of them. And what were we talking about? The strange and exotic romance of the school librarian.

"Stephen? Once more?" Ellie sat beside Miss Billingham, on whose face could now be seen the dabs of make-up which announced the return of good times.

"She didn't care about the match at all," said Tara loudly. "She was just thinking of her bloomin' boyfriend."

"That's not quite fair," said Miss Billingham. "I'm delighted about your football. And I really hope you win. And . . ." She blushed. "And so does Stephen."

"But why did you say you could see him once more?" asked Ellie.

Miss Billingham sighed. "There are one or two things I

haven't told you about Stephen and me," she said. "Things you might find slightly shocking."

OK, so now we were really listening.

Speaking in a low monotone, and darting occasional glances in the direction of the oldies at the back of the bus, Miss Billingham quietly revealed the previously censored bits of her great story – the bit that took place after her beloved Stephen had left for the country and got married.

"I wrote letters," Miss Billingham said suddenly. "Birthday cards. Valentines."

"Miss B." Eve sounded genuinely shocked. "But he was married."

"I loved him. Sometimes I called him on the telephone. If she answered, I'd hang up straight away. If it was Stephen, I'd listen to him saying, 'Hello? Hello?' as if he really didn't know who it was. Then I'd put the receiver down."

"Wasn't that kind of destructive?" I asked.

Miss Billingham shrugged. "I needed to hear his voice. I was missing him."

"Yes, but—"

"You wouldn't understand!" she snapped suddenly. "It wasn't my fault the marriage went wrong. She probably would have left him anyway. She became convinced that I was still seeing him."

"You destroyed their marriage," said Eve.

"If you know you're meant to be with someone, the usual rules don't apply." Miss Billingham spoke with quiet, fanatical conviction.

"You weren't responsible either," I said. "You don't believe in nice-girl rules any more than we do."

Miss Billingham smiled and gazed out of the window.

Ahead of us, we saw the outskirts of Oakmere. It had seemed a good idea to get Miss Billingham talking to take our minds off the game ahead but I guess none of us was exactly reassured by what we were discovering. I mean, how would you feel if your quiet, innocent school librarian suddenly revealed herself to be a secret love-hooligan, a marriage-breaker, a crazed telephone pest?

"So now's happy-ever-after time?" asked Roberta.

"Stephen has the children. His wife lives in the north. He says that, if he sees me too much, he'll lose custody of them. His wife is . . ." Miss Billingham hesitated, " . . . a rather vengeful woman."

We were approaching the bus station. Standing up, we reached for our kitbags, each of us kind of stunned by what we had heard.

"He'll come to the match," said Miss Billingham. "You'll have two supporters at least."

"Terrific," said Lisa.

CHAPTER FOURTEEN

Moving the Goalposts

Bottom line, we hadn't realized the tournament would be such a big deal. As we approached the ground, we could see teams in different strips – mostly boys but also a few girls – warming up on the two pitches. Although the official starting time was still forty-five minutes away, spectators were already standing on the touchlines, chatting and laughing in the sunshine.

Miss Billingham had gone to fetch the love of her life, so that, arriving to register the team in the clubhouse, we were without adult support when we most needed it.

"Hotshots?" Gibson, now in a smart blue blazer, was behind the desk. He looked up at us as if we were the girls' team sent from hell. "You withdrew. You're meant to be back in London."

"No," said Lisa, putting on her most winning smile. "We were asked whether we wanted to withdraw. We decided that we don't."

The organizer was looking down at his team sheets, shaking his head.

"Sir, we've come a long way for this," I said. "We just want to play some football."

"It's not the football that's the problem. It's everything else. Is there an adult who's looking after you?"

We glanced at one another. "She's kind of busy at present," I said. "She'll be along later."

"Here's what we'll do." The man was smiling broadly as if together we had somehow found a solution to his problem. "I can give your team an Oakmere FC pennant and each of you a tournament medal. And we'll fix up a match for the future. When things have settled down."

"Excuse me, we've come here to play in a tournament," said Eve. "We don't want medals unless we've earned them."

"And we don't want to come back," muttered Roberta.

"I was hoping you'd meet us halfway on this." Gibson spoke briskly, abandoning the pretence of friendliness. "All we're asking is that you help us avoid trouble."

For a brief moment, there was silence and I sensed a weakening of resolve among the Hotshots. Maybe Gibson was right, and the decent, responsible thing to do was to meet him halfway, take the medals and head on home. Then I thought of the card from our parents.

"It wasn't us who caused trouble," I said with quiet determination. "If we don't play, the bullies have won."

"We've done nothing wrong, sir," Charlie said reasonably.

Gibson thought for a moment. Then, sighing tragically, he looked down at the papers in front of him. "Your first round will luckily be on one of the outside pitches, away from most of the spectators. If you win that, you'll be in the girls' final. Personally, I hope you don't win." He glanced down at the list of our names in front of him. "By the way, who are your substitutes?"

"Substitutes?" said Lisa. "We've got five players and two substitutes."

"Five?" Gibson laughed. "Didn't you read the rules? This is a seven-a-side tournament. All the other squads have ten players."

We looked at one another in amazement.

"Still want to play?" Gibson asked.

"Sure," I said. "Why not?"

"I don't believe this."

Lisa spoke for us all as we changed into our kit in the tent set aside for visitors. It wasn't just that the organizers had tried to stop us playing – we were used to opposition, after all. No, it was that last bombshell that had reduced us all to silence.

Seven-a-side. We looked over at the pitches that had been marked out. They were bigger than we were used to and the goals were almost full-sized. Playing two extra players on a large pitch changed the game completely. Fitness would be everything – and we didn't even have any substitutes to replace tired or injured players.

"They must have sent the rules to school," said Ellie gloomily. "Trust Morley to forget to give them to us."

"Maybe we'll get beaten in the first match," said Lisa. "That would solve their little problem."

"So what's the game plan?" I asked. "I mean, who plays where in seven-a-side?"

We talked it through. Some players had a natural position – Tara in goal, Charlie in defence, Lisa as striker – but, of the rest, we had two regulars, Roberta and me, and two players who normally came on as substitutes. In the end, we opted for a strong defence of Charlie and Roberta, with me in midfield, playing between Ellie and Eve, with Lisa the lone striker up front. It meant that we were vulnerable down the flanks but there was nothing we could do about that.

Emerging from the tent, we made our way to the pitch furthest away from the clubhouse. Miss Billingham was standing on the touchline.

"Where's Stephen?" asked Eve.

"He's coming later. He'll see you in the next match."

"What next match?" Lisa laughed humourlessly. "It's a knockout tournament. We'll be lucky to get through this one."

"They've cheated us, Miss B," said Tara. "Changed the rules to seven-a-side."

"Let's warm up," I said quickly. "Kick-off's in five minutes."

"What about a team talk, Miss B?" asked Roberta. "Like, tactics?"

Miss Billingham gave a quiet little smile. "Just . . . be there for each other," she said.

As we jogged over towards our goal, I glanced at the opposition. They wore a dazzling all-white kit with the name of their sponsors, Oscar Videos, in bright green across the front.

"What d'you think?" asked Lisa, adjusting her captain's armband.

"No problem." I smiled. "Remember the golden rule – the flasher the kit, the lamer the team."

Lisa laughed. "Let's hope you're right," she said.

Sometimes you play in a match that has a strange, unreal atmosphere to it. This was one of those. There were only a few spectators watching and my hunch had been right – the opposition team, from a local village called Thurston, looked good but were nervy players who hung back from tackles and hardly talked to one another at all during the match.

An easy win for the Hotshots? Er, not exactly.

We played like a team that hadn't even been thinking about football for weeks. Sure we passed and, sure, Lisa made a few jinking runs but there was no edge to our play, no hunger for victory. Soon it was Thurston who began to look as if they believed they could win.

Twice, a lunging tackle from Charlie saved us from going a goal down. On another occasion, Roberta and Ellie went for the same ball, clattered into one another, leaving one of Thurston's strikers clear on goal. Luckily for us, she panicked and sent the ball over the crossbar. By the time the half-time whistle blew, we were hanging on for survival.

In the past, a few words from our coach Gerry Phelan would have fired us up, but now we stood in a circle, gloomily silent. Even Tara, who could usually be depended upon to make us laugh, seemed preoccupied, her thoughts elsewhere.

113

"These guys are so rubbish." In the end, it was me who broke the silence. "All we have to do is play our normal game and we'll be all over them."

"Yeah, like we really believe that," said Lisa.

"Come on!" I found myself saying angrily. "Think what we've been through to get here. After all that, you want us to go out like wimps? That's what they're expecting. At least, if we get beaten in the final, we'll know we've given it our best shot. We're playing like we actually want to lose."

"We haven't had one shot on goal," said Eve.

"Yeah, and whose fault is that?" snapped Lisa. "I'm getting no service from the midfield. I can't do it on my own and as for you on the wing—"

"None of us can do it on our own," I said, as the referee blew his whistle to mark the end of half-time. "Come on, this isn't for the school or for our parents. This one's for us, right?"

We jogged back into our positions. Beside me, Ellie smiled. "Great speech, Stevie," she said. "For a moment there, I almost believed you."

I laughed. The whistle blew.

It had been their kick-off but, maybe because she was annoyed with me, Lisa went for the Thurston player who had the ball like a hunger-crazed lion attacking its prey. There was a crunch as they made contact and I was faintly aware of protests from the Thurston players as the ball ricocheted back to me. In that split-second, I seemed to hear Gerry's voice in my head – "Play the whistle" – and, while the Thurston girls were looking at the referee, waiting for him to award a free kick, I passed the ball out to Ellie. She ran a few steps down the wing, then sent a hopeful ball into the centre where – could I believe my eyes? – little Eve had appeared out of nowhere. It was difficult to tell who was panicking the worse – Eve or the Thurston goalkeeper who rushed out towards her. Eve flailed a foot in the general direction of the ball and somehow found contact. Low and fast, it went through the goalkeeper's legs and into the net.

For a few seconds, there was so little reaction from the crowd that I thought the goal must have been disallowed by the referee, but then he pointed to the centre circle. It was at that moment that we all noticed for the first time that Lisa was still on the ground, clutching her ankle.

By the time play started again, a couple of minutes later, Lisa had hobbled off the pitch, leaving us with six players. Suddenly Thurston had come alive, screaming at the referee every time we tackled one of their players, pouring forward in attack.

"I'm coming back into defence," I screamed at Charlie. "We've got to hold on."

How we managed to survive those last minutes, I'll never know. Desperate for a goal, Thurston hurried their shots. Charlie was rock-like between Roberta and me in defence. Tara made save after save. Ellie and Eve buzzed around in the midfield, occasionally getting the ball and taking it towards the Thurston goal, more as a tactic for wasting time than in any serious hopes of increasing our lead.

When the final whistle blew, I sank to my knees, exhausted but triumphant. 1–0 against bad opposition. It was not exactly a glorious victory – the Hotshots had never played worse, to tell the truth – but we were through to the final.

Tara placed a hand on my shoulder. "Well played, Yank," she said.

I smiled up at her. "We're still standing," I said. I looked over to where Lisa was lying back on the grass, covering her face with her hand as the manager of the Thurston team looked at her ankle. "At least, most of us are."

CHAPTER FIFTEEN

Crunch

Considering we had played badly and won, considering we had managed to reach the final, considering there had been none of the crowd trouble we had been told to expect, the mood among the Hotshots was kind of subdued after the game.

We were tired, our striker had a swollen ankle and wasn't exactly doing the silent hero act – I guess each of us, in our heart of hearts, was thinking of that train back home. We had played some football. We had even won. Right now, that seemed more than enough.

We sat in the shade of a tree, away from the pitches where the boys were playing their matches. At one point, Charlie wandered over to the clubhouse to discover who we were to play in the final. It was the Oakmere team, who had won their match 5–0.

"Great," said Roberta. "We're playing the home team."

"And they've just scored five goals." Ellie sighed. "This could be embarrassing."

As the day grew warmer, crowds were gathering around the larger pitches – crowds of strangers, who'd soon be cheering on the team against us. For the first time, the

Hotshots would be going into a big game without a manager, without friends or even parents on the touchline. It was a weird feeling.

Our one supporter, Miss Billingham, appeared. By the look of her – the way she walked, the little smile on her face – she had found her beloved Stephen.

"Well done, girls," she said. "One–love. Very good."

"It's one–nil," said Roberta, adding quietly, "Someone's got love on the brain."

"Stephen says you'll beat Oakmere. They're strong but you've got more skill."

None of us replied.

"He's over there, actually." Miss Billingham looked round and waved like a little girl at a tall man with long grey hair and a beard who stood about fifty metres away. I recognized the romantic reader from the pond. As he walked slowly towards us, I had to admit he looked kind of striking – like some character out of the Old Testament or something – but a love object, the man who had changed Miss Billingham's life? As Tara would say, it was beyond weird.

"Hi." He stood beside Miss Billingham. "Well done in the match. I caught the last couple of minutes."

"Thank you," said Eve.

He looked down at Lisa's ankle which had been bandaged in the ambulance tent. "Are you going to be able to play?"

Lisa shook her head. "It's a sprain but it's really painful."

"You should start the game at least. If you're a player down at kick-off, they'll have a psychological advantage."

"You've seen them play?" I asked.

118

Stephen nodded. "Several times. They're keen but they aren't as experienced as you. Look out for their number five. She's the only one who scores goals for them."

"Is it worth putting a marker on her?" I asked.

"I think so. She burns a short fuse – gets frustrated easily."

Miss Billingham had laid a basket on the ground and was taking out sandwiches. "Let's talk tactics over lunch," she said happily. "I've got a feeling this is going to be the Hotshots' finest hour."

"Yeah, as if," said Roberta, and all of us, even Lisa, managed to laugh.

As soon as the announcement for the match was made, we knew that we were in for a tough game.

"Ten minutes to go before the final of the Oakmere Girls' Under-14 Cup. The finalists are . . ." The announcer paused briefly. "Oakmere Junior Ladies!" There were cheers from the main pitch where the crowd was already gathering. "Against them, all the way from London, the Hotshots."

And suddenly, a sound we had never heard in any of our previous games was echoing around the ground – a loud booing.

We looked at one another in amazement. "Charming," said Roberta with a nervous smile.

Miss Billingham's boyfriend Stephen stood up and looked towards the pitch. "It's just one section of the crowd," he said. "Bunch of teenagers who hang around the town causing trouble. They don't matter."

"We're guests," said Eve in a shocked voice. "It's not exactly sporting, is it?"

Stephen laughed. "I'll accompany you to the pitch," he said. "Then you can let your feet do the talking."

Staying close to the tall figure of Stephen, we made our way towards the main pitch. Although he looked kind of weird and shaggy, there was something reassuring about the guy. Over lunch, we had been able to talk our game-plan through with him. We had decided that, even though Lisa could hardly run, she would play up front for as long as possible. Ellie was going to close down their one dangerous player, the number five. We'd play defensively and hope to score on the break.

A new chorus of boos announced our arrival on the pitch – there were probably around thirty bikers and their friends standing near the halfway line. The rest of the crowd was looking at them with some confusion.

"One thing," said Stephen over the noise. "Just play football. Don't let them rattle you – whatever they do." He smiled. "Good luck."

"Oh *yes*!" Miss Billingham clasped her hands together in front of her. "Come on, you Hotshots."

We jogged onto the pitch. The bikers chanted, "What a load of rubbish!" On the nearside of the pitch, I noticed the familiar figure of Mrs Pritchard, seated on a small chair between Mr and Mrs Fairbrother. "We've got one other supporter," I shouted to Ellie as Mrs Pritchard waved at us with both arms. Her daughter said something to her but the old woman kept waving.

There was a tap on my shoulder. It was Lisa, holding out

the captain's armband to me. "Here," she said. "We need a captain with two legs."

"Me?" I looked in astonishment at Lisa who had never previously been famous for heroic unselfish gestures.

"Just for one game," she said. "You deserve it." She turned to the other Hotshots. "Stevie's captain," she shouted.

"Yo – the Yank!" Tara punched the air.

The referee was standing on the centre spot. He blew his whistle. I ran towards him as we took our positions. Their captain, a powerfully built dark-haired girl, the famous number five, extended a hand. With a dangerous smile, she said, "You're dead meat, suckers."

I glanced at the referee, a neat, athletic-looking man in his early thirties.

"Now now, Paula. Remember what we said in training."

Eh, what was that? I looked from one to the other, realization dawning. The referee was only their coach – that was all we needed. He tossed a coin. The Ladies won and elected to kick off. With a little wink in the direction of his team, the referee blew his whistle. The crowd cheered.

This was going to be a tough one.

The pattern of the game, both on the pitch and off, was quickly established. Oakmere Junior Ladies were not exactly ladylike – they were bigger than us and had obviously decided that the best way to beat us was by using their size and strength, barging us off the ball, delivering heavy tackles whenever they could. As for the crowd, all we could hear were cheers when Oakmere had the ball, boos when we were in possession.

In the first two minutes, Roberta had been brought down by a scything tackle, and Charlie had found herself in the middle of a painful Oakmere sandwich just after she had passed the ball. Most spectacularly of all, little Eve had almost been sent into orbit when the number five crashed into her.

As the referee checked whether Eve was all right, I began to see how we could win this game. Bigstuff and his leather-jacketed goons were laughing and jeering with every tackle that Oakmere delivered but already other people in the crowd were looking at them with open disapproval.

As for the Junior Ladies, they were so fired up by the noise and the atmosphere that they were forgetting to play football. Sooner or later later, the ref – even this ref – would have to step in to warn them. Our job was to keep cool, play football – as Stephen said, let our feet do the talking.

But soon we were in trouble. After Eve had groggily regained her feet, Charlie sent the free kick to Lisa who turned to make a run, then crumpled to the ground. I ran over to her.

"Can't go on," she gasped.

As Ellie helped her off the field, the mood of the crowd changed further. Several spectators clapped, drowning out the jeers of the bikers.

"Sub?" the referee called out to me.

"We haven't got a sub," I shouted back.

The ref raised his eyebrows in surprise and the game started with a drop ball between Roberta and their number five.

Too late I saw the danger. Ellie hadn't returned to her position, so that when Oakmere's captain skipped past Roberta, she was clear on goal without her marker in sight. Charlie sprinted across to cover but the number five checked, then let fly a shot for goal. It took a deflection off Charlie's leg and there was nothing that Tara could do to prevent a goal.

The jeers and chants from Bigstuff and his gang were deafening.

1–0 down and a player short.

We re-started, Roberta passing to me. I dwelt on the ball for a second, glanced towards Ellie – and felt a searing pain as someone hit the back of my right ankle, studs first.

For a few moments, as I lay on the ground, all I could think of was that I was out of the match. I was aware of the sound of the crowd, angry and restless. I closed my eyes – round here, it seemed, they even booed you for being fouled. I looked up. A few yards away, the referee was reaching into the back pocket of his black shorts. As he held up a yellow card in front of their number five, who shook her head in disbelief, some of the crowd clapped.

"Do that once more, Paula, and I'll send you off," the ref shouted.

I stood up and tried my ankle. It was still painful but nothing was broken. As I hobbled a few steps, spectators around the ground applauded.

Charlie put a hand on my shoulder. "That's one way of getting the crowd on our side," she said. "You going to be OK?"

"I guess."

The referee joined us. "Take your time," he said with

what was almost a smile. "If you have to go off too, we'll have a riot on our hands."

The movement was coming back to my ankle. "You stopped the clock, right?"

He laughed. "Of course."

"I'm OK. Let's go."

The referee blew. Roberta took the free kick, passing it to Ellie. For the first time Oakmere were hanging back, as if afraid to do anything that would set the crowd going once more. As for me, I was still having difficulty running. After two minutes of careful defensive play by both sides, the referee blew for half-time.

Lisa hobbled on to the pitch to join us.

"These guys are beyond violent," said Tara, punching her gloved right fist into the palm of her left hand. "We gotta dish it out or we're finished."

"No way." I shook my head. "They've played into our hands. The crowd are behind us now. If we just play football, keep it cool, we can get back into this game."

"But we're a player short," said Roberta.

A thought occurred to me. I turned to Lisa. "How d'you like the idea of playing in goal?"

The team looked at me in astonishment.

"Oakmere are just going to defend," I said. "Even if Lisa can't run, she can use her hands. Tara can take her place up front."

"Cunning," said Roberta.

"It's either brilliant or dumb," said Charlie. "Let's do it."

All eyes turned to Lisa. She milked the moment like a

124

true drama queen for a few seconds, then gave a dramatic little nod of agreement.

"OK, change shirts," I said.

"Er, no way am I doing a striptease in the middle of the pitch," said Tara.

Laughing, we gathered round and, with great difficulty, Lisa and Tara managed the swap. When the whistle blew to mark the end of half-time, the old Hotshots spirit had put the smile back on our faces. Anyone just arriving at the game would have thought it was our team that had the 1–0 lead.

"Our injured player's back on," I told the ref. "We've changed keepers."

He glanced towards Lisa and nodded. "Good thinking," he murmured.

We kicked off for the second half, playing with new confidence. Tara passed to Ellie who switched the ball across to Roberta as she made a run down the left. She skipped past their right back and only a desperate tackle from Oakmere's other defender prevented her from being on goal. The two Oakmere players screamed angrily at one another.

Roberta took the throw, aiming the ball at the towering figure of Tara who flicked the ball on with her head into the area. Their goalkeeper went for it but, under pressure from Ellie, fumbled. By a miracle the ball fell to me. Quick glance at goal. Outside of the foot – and the crowd erupted. 1–1.

Suddenly there was only one side in it. Again and again, we attacked with Tara using her strength to get through the defence. At our end, Oakmere tried the occasional, unconvincing long shot at goal which merely allowed Lisa to hop about dramatically and remind the crowd of her unbelievable heroism.

But no more goals. Time ticked by. During a break in play, I asked the referee if extra time would be played if it was all square at full-time. He shook his head. "Penalty shoot-out," he said.

Uh-oh. Knowing the way the rules went round here, they wouldn't let us change keepers. A one-legged goalkeeper in a shoot-out? If it came to that, we'd be finished.

"We need to score," I screamed.

Gradually Oakmere were coming back into the game. Eager to get forward, Ellie was forgetting that she was supposed to be marking the number five. During one of Tara's runs forward, the ball was quickly thrown out by their goalkeeper to the one person who could still turn the match in their favour. She dummied, then skipped past me. Charlie held back, not wanting to lunge in, but the number five passed to her right, ran round Charlie to take the return ball and sent a rocket of a shot towards goal.

I guess I have to admit that this was Lisa's finest hour. Somehow, despite her bad leg, she dived to her right and not only made a save but kept the ball. She rolled it out to Charlie, who turned and threaded a perfect pass through the opposition defence.

Tara was there, advancing on the opposition goal. It was time for a cool finish and Tara isn't exactly famous for being cool. Yet, just as their goalkeeper came out to meet her, she gave a little shimmy, then, as the keeper went down for a shot that never came, ran around her, to sidefoot the ball into the net.

2–1. A minute to go. We fell back in defence but

somehow the fight had gone out of Oakmere. When the final whistle blew, I fell on the ground, aware only of a huge sense of relief. Somewhere in the distance, the crowd was clapping and it seemed I could hear the voice of Mrs Pritchard. "Well done, girls," she was shouting again and again.

We had done it.

The crowd were still applauding as a tall, balding man in a dark suit walked on to the pitch, carrying a small silver cup.

"And here to present the trophy," said the announcer over the loudspeaker, "Bryan Gunn of Norwich City."

For some reason, the tall man decided first to congratulate Lisa who had moved into her full smiling-through-tears-of-pain number. "So who's the captain?" he asked.

I stepped forward, shook his hand, and took the cup.

"I think you're expected to do a lap of honour," said Bryan Gunn. Leaving one-legged Lisa in the centre circle, we jogged around the pitch, past Bigstuff and his gang who stood in silence, past Miss Billingham and Stephen, past the Fairbrothers and Mrs Pritchard.

At first, we thought the two policemen who stood at one end of the pitch were there to cheer us on our way. That was until one of them stepped out of the crowd and beckoned to Tara.

"Game's over, young lady," he said with a grim little smile. "It's time for you to come with us."

127

CHAPTER SIXTEEN

City Kids

It wasn't exactly the last word in celebration parties.

An hour later, we were back in the sitting room at Cholmondley Manor. No one had told us why the police wanted to talk to Tara but, to judge from the expression on the faces of Mr and Mrs Fairbrother, it was serious.

Mrs Pritchard was trying to ease the atmosphere by asking us about the game but, by now, football was the last thing on our minds. Even before she had been asked to accompany Tara and the two policemen to Tara's room, Miss Billingham had not exactly been a tower of strength. The fact that Stephen hadn't been allowed to stay with her had done nothing for her composure – I guess theirs hadn't exactly been the last lovers' farewell she had had in mind.

"We're taking this young lady down to the station for questioning." The older of the two policemen stood at the door. "We'll be as quick as we can so that the rest of you can get back to London tonight."

Tara was standing miserably between the two policemen. "Tell them, Stevie," she pleaded. "Tell them I'm not a liar."

"Officer, I've been with Tara all day," I pleaded. "She's done nothing wrong."

"We're taking her down to the station to take a statement," said one of the policemen. "It's a matter of theft."

"Someone's planted the gear on me!" Tara shouted. "All the stuff stolen from Mrs P has been put in my—"

"That's enough!" snapped the policeman. "You're in enough trouble without trying to influence witnesses."

I stood up. "Sir, this morning we saw the stolen shotguns in a shed. I can show you where it is."

The policeman nodded patronizingly. "You can include all that in your statement, miss, but you should bear in mind that hindering the police in the pursuit of their inquiries is a criminal offence." He turned to where Mrs Fairbrother was standing. "Thank you, madam," he said. "One of my colleagues will return soon."

"Thank you, officer," said Mrs Fairbrother.

I couldn't help it. After Tara had left with the policemen, I suddenly found my eyes were full of tears. "It's true about the shed," I said to Mrs Pritchard. "You believe me, don't you?"

The old woman looked confused. "I don't know what to believe," she said.

As if I hadn't spoken, Mrs Fairbrother laid a hand on Mrs Pritchard's arm. "I'm sorry about this, mother," she said. "You've had an awful time. I feel responsible, having suggested this visit. I should have known that there would be too much temptation for these . . . city kids."

"Mrs Fairbrother, it's all been a misunderstanding," said Eve. "Surely you see that."

129

"Let's just hope they aren't all involved." Mr Fairbrother spoke in a low, conversational voice.

"Hm." Mrs Fairbrother glanced at Mrs Pritchard significantly. "Maybe it's time you girls packed your cases."

I was about to mention the shed again but it was clear now that nothing any of us said would change the Fairbrothers' minds. We were just city kids, after all. It was too late for words now. Action was needed.

Silently, the six of us trooped out of the sitting room. As the others made their way up the stairs, I hung back – then cut back to the kitchen and out of the back door.

I ran through the garden, past the farm buildings, up the slight incline of the path which led up the hill to the rabbit field. Breathing heavily, I opened the gate and turned right.

For the first time for days, clouds filled the sky and, although it was still early evening, there was a quiet, oppressive gloom to the countryside.

Two hundred yards. I looked down to the right. There was no sign of life from the Walkers' cottage. Crouching low in the grass I ran the last fifty yards to the shed.

Peering through the window, I could see little change. Then, glancing down to the cottage to check that I wasn't being watched, I moved around to the door. The chain and padlock had gone. I turned the handle and opened the door.

The shed was narrow and about three metres long. Its gloomy interior had a dry, musty smell to it and, before I could stop myself, I coughed loudly. I shut the door and, in the semi-darkness, groped around the walls, along the floor, in every dusty corner. There was a square metal bin in the far corner. I was groping behind it when I became aware that the shed had become lighter. A gust of wind must have opened the door behind me.

Except there was no wind that evening.

Slowly, I withdrew my arm and, still kneeling in the dirt, turned towards the light. In the doorway was the giant shadow of a man. He was holding something, pointing it at me.

"Looking for this, were you?"

It was Walker's voice. In his hand, pointing down at me, was one of Mrs Pritchard's shotguns.

"I dropped something," I said. "A sort of bracelet."

"Get up. And don't try anything stupid."

I tried a smile. "I'm not that dumb."

"It was dumb to come looking for the guns," he said slowly. "I told you. Accidents happen in the countryside."

I felt sweat running down my back as I looked up the twin barrels of the shotgun. "Accidents?"

"Yeah." He leant against the side of the door. "Say we wait a bit longer. It's getting dark. Say I see a figure creeping about the place in the shadows. Say I decide to do my job – protect Mrs Pritchard's property. I fetch the old shooter and . . ." With his thumb, Walker pushed forward a catch on the gun. "Bang. Poachers, see. I'm paid to look out for poachers."

"And shoot them?"

Walker shrugged. "People are more understanding about that sort of thing out here. Nobody likes poachers."

"Would they be so understanding if they knew you'd been in prison?"

He straightened, suddenly tense.

131

"Yes." I spoke more loudly, but there was a tremor in my voice. "We know all about you, Paul."

OK, so it was crazy but, right then, staring down the barrel of a gun held by a psycho, I hadn't exactly got much to lose. Walker needed to know that we had a weapon too.

"For example, we know why you're here," I said as calmly as I could manage. "Years ago, you were sent to prison by Mr Fairbrother for thieving. Stealing Mrs Pritchard's property was your way of making money and getting a bit of revenge."

"Eh?" There was a sort of evil chuckle from Walker. "Is that the sort of logic they teach you at school?" He took a step closer and placed the cold metal of the gun barrel against my forehead. "I'm now going to make you a promise," he said quietly. "If you say one word of this to anyone, I'll come looking for you in London. Understand?"

I nodded.

"Revenge?" He gave another laugh. "It was the Fairbrothers who hired us, you silly little girl."

"I don't understand."

"They want the house. They want that old hag Pritchard in an old folks' home but she refuses to go. So . . ." he shrugged. "There's nothing like a bit of burglary and harassment from kids to remind an old party what a big, bad world it is and how vulnerable she is."

"What harassment? Who were the kids?"

"You. That's why you're here. Mrs Fairbrother set up the visit because she thought seven girls from the smoke running riot would finish the job off. Drive the old girl bonkers."

For some reason, Roberta's favourite word came into my

mind. "Charming," I said. "It was you I saw downstairs that night, wasn't it?"

In reply, Walker gave a heartless laugh. "Every day, some of her possessions went missing. Sometimes we put things back. See, Mrs P? It was there all the time. No wonder she thought she was losing it."

"Poor Pilchard." For a moment, I forgot my own plight as I saw the old woman's confused, anxious face in my mind's eye. All she had wanted was to stay in the house where she had lived for years.

"So, little girl." Walker prodded my head with the gun. "Will you be running back to the house and keeping your mouth shut or is there going to be a little accident?"

"I . . ." Maybe it was sweat running down the side of my face, maybe it was tears that filled my eyes. "I'm going back," I said. "I'll forget all about this. Bottom line, I just want to go home to my parents." He lowered the gun and, breathing heavily, I stood up.

It was at that moment that I heard an oddly familiar snuffling sound. A small, dark shape appeared behind Walker. Bournville. Behind him, holding on to his lead, was Mrs Pritchard.

"Hello, Walker," she said quietly. "You found my shotguns after all, then."

"Yes, ma'am." For a moment it was as if Walker couldn't remember which part to play – psycho or servant.

"I heard every word you said," said Mrs Pritchard calmly. Ignoring me now, Walker raised the shotgun to his shoulder and levelled it at Mrs Pritchard.

"You silly man." Without a moment's hesitation, the old woman moved forward, leaning heavily on her walking stick. "How would you explain that shooting me was an accident? Do I look like a poacher? And what was my stolen Purdey doing in your hand?"

"It wasn't me," said Walker in a defeated voice. "Wasn't my idea."

Mrs Pritchard was standing in front of him, no more than a metre from the barrel of the gun. "I know." She smiled sadly. "It wasn't you. It was my own daughter." She extended her hand. Walker slowly lowered the gun and, shaking his head as if he couldn't believe that he had been on the brink of murder, handed it to Mrs Pritchard.

She opened it briskly, and took out the two cartridges. "Safety catch was off, too," she said, almost cheerfully. "The thing could have gone off at any time."

Charming.

It was the strangest of evenings at Cholmondley Manor. The Walkers were formally charged with theft and taken away by the police. Mr and Mrs Fairbrother were required to give statements and told Mrs Pritchard they would be driving back to London that night. They didn't say goodbye to us.

At about seven, Tara returned in a police car, stepping out and punching the air joyfully. Even PC Smethurst, who had driven her back, allowed himself a tight little smile before driving off.

So, once again, it was just the seven Hotshots, Miss Billingham and Mrs Pritchard around the kitchen table that night, munching the last of the dry cheddar cheese in the fridge.

We tried to talk of the tournament but somehow football paled into insignificance beside the events of that evening.

"If it hadn't been for Stevie, they might have got away with it," Lisa said at one point. "Tara would probably be in jail."

"No way," Tara snapped. "I sorted those guys out at the police station, no worries. I told them the Psychos had planted that gear in my room."

"You were beyond scared," said Charlie.

"Shut up scared!"

But behind the jokes and the laughter, we knew that, when we went home tomorrow, we would be leaving a problem behind us.

"What will you do about the house, Mrs P?" asked Ellie at one point.

"I'm not going into a home. They wanted to force me out but I'm staying here. Cholmondley is my life."

"Yes, but who'll take the place of the Walkers?" asked Roberta. "Who'll look after you?"

Mrs Pritchard frowned. "Can't pay anyone. It's just a cottage and a living allowance. Who would possibly want to live out here in the middle of nowhere, looking after an old woman?"

There was a long silence. Then, as if at a signal, each of us found ourselves turning to Miss Billingham.

She gave an odd, slightly embarrassed smile. "I think I might know someone who could help," she said quietly.

"Yo." Roberta held up her hand. "Another winning goal."

I slapped her palm with mine, giving her a high five. "Hotshot power," I said.

Cholmondley Manor Cottage

Dear Stevie

Thank you for your letter. I think that maybe we're now past the "Miss Billingham" stage, don't you? "Diana" will do very nicely.

You asked me what has happened here during the long months since the Hotshots' famous visit. The answer is: quite a lot!

I've only seen the loathsome Walker couple once. I accompanied Daphne Pritchard to the local magistrates' court where she had to give evidence in the case against Paul James Walker. As you might have heard, he was found guilty and sentenced to six months in jail. Jill Walker has returned to London and I hope and pray that that is the last we ever ever see of them!!

The Fairbrothers are not exactly popular around here. According to the police, they weren't actually guilty enough to take them to court, although a lot of people have been saying that if trying to make life so unpleasant for your own mum that she's forced to go into an old people's home and leave you the house doesn't make you guilty of something, then it's a funny old world. Of course, the fact that Mr Fairbrother is a magistrate might pos-sibly have helped keep them out of court – nobody ever said life was fair, Stevie . . .

Anyway, what Daphne finds most shocking is that her own daughter thought that those "charming little girls" would help her decide that she was too old to be living alone. (If only she knew!!!)

We get on really well. I spend much of my time down at the manor and we talk about all sorts of things. Daphne is not a great reader of books – a copy of The Field *is about her limit – but she's a good listener and we have long talks. Recently I've been doing a bit of freelance work for the local newspaper, which helps on the money side.*

Oh well, I suppose I'd better tell you my big news. Stephen and I are engaged. His worries about his children not liking their dad having a girlfriend turned out to be poppycock (surprise surprise!) and having a free cottage to live in at Cholmondley Manor will give us a great start. Daphne was a little fierce towards him at first and told him he was much too old to have long hair, but they get on well now.

Do I miss Broadhurst? Just now and then. It's not the staff or the work but you children who used to make me laugh every day. If there's anyone to thank for what has happened to me, it's the seven of you – plus Jamie, in the background, of course.

The other evening, I had been reading to Stephen and we switched on the television news. Some election was happening somewhere – the candidates who were standing were described as a "dream team".

It reminded me of you lot – the Hotshots.

In the end, you remembered the only bit of coaching advice I ever gave you. You were there for each other – and you were there for us, too. By doing that, you taught a few grown-ups a lesson about loyalty and friendship.

June wedding? Are you up for it? I thought about

having a couple of Hotshots bridesmaids but then I just can't get my head around the idea of Tara in a fluffy bridesmaid's dress.

As you might say . . .

Er, I don't think so.

Much love

Diana